BUNTER THE RACKETEER

D1376350

© FLEETWAY PUBLICATIONS LTD. 1965

This edition of Bunter The Racketeer was
first published in 1965 by May Fair Books
Ltd., 14 St. James's Place, London S.W.1,
and was printed in Great Britain by Love &
Malcomson Ltd., Brighton Road, Redhill,
Surrey.

CONDITIONS OF SALE: This book is sold subject to the condition that
it shall not, by way of trade or otherwise, be lent, re-sold, hired out or
otherwise circulated without the publisher's prior consent in any form of
binding or cover other than that in which it is published and without a similar
condition including this condition being imposed on the subsequent purchaser.

FRANK RICHARDS

Bunter
the Racketeer

COVER ILLUSTRATION
BY MARY GERNATT

Armada

A horrified squeak escaped Bunter, as he felt himself going.

Bricks for Bunter!

"SAFE enough here——"
   "Not if Bunter spots it!"
   "Oh, that's all right!"
   Billy Bunter grinned.

The door of Study No. 1 in the Remove passage at Greyfriars was half-open. Billy Bunter was about a foot from the door. So every word spoken in the study came quite clearly to the fat ears of the Owl of the Remove.

The five fellows in the study did not seem to be aware that William George Bunter was just outside. At any rate, they spoke as freely as though there were no fat ears to hear.

Bob Cherry had dumped a large parcel on the study table. It was wrapped in brown paper, tied with plenty of string with many knots. Billy Bunter did not need telling what that parcel contained. He knew that there was to be a picnic on Popper's Island, up the river, that afternoon.

"Leave it here," went on Bob. "It will be all right while we're seeing about the boat."

"But if Bunter sees it——" said Frank Nugent.

"Well, if he does, he won't know what's in it."

"No; that's so."

Billy Bunter, in the passage, winked. He was quite amused.

"Come on, then!" said Harry Wharton.

Billy Bunter moved quickly away from the door. He

was two or three yards off when the chums of the Remove emerged from Study No. 1.

He blinked at them through his big spectacles as they passed him, going towards the stairs.

"I say, you fellows!" squeaked Bunter.

"Can't stop!" said Bob.

"Oh, really, Cherry——"

"Ladies to meet," explained Bob. "They're pretty certain to be late; but we mustn't be, not even for the pleasure of hearing you wag your chin, old fat man."

"I say, if you fellows would like me to come——"

"Jolly big 'if'!" remarked Johnny Bull.

"The likefulness would be terrific," declared Hurree Jamset Ram Singh. "But the objectfulness of the esteemed Marjorie and the beauteous Clara would be enormous."

"Oh, all right!" said Bunter scornfully. "I know you don't want me about when there are girls present. It's rather mean to be jealous of a fellow's good looks."

"Oh, my hat!"

"Ha, ha, ha!"

"You can cackle," said Bunter. "But if you think Marjorie would take any notice of you when I'm present, it only shows what conceited asses you are. You can cackle."

"Thanks!" said Bob. "We will. Ha, ha, ha!"

The fat junior watched them till they disappeared. Then he blinked out of the landing window, and spotted them again in the quad, going down to the gates.

He grinned.

The coast was clear now. Billy Bunter rolled up the passage again to Study No. 1.

He rolled into that study and fixed his eyes and his spectacles on the big parcel on the table.

As it was only a couple of hours since dinner, and he had eaten only enough for three or four fellows, Bunter naturally was hungry. He was tempted to open that parcel, and begin on its contents on the spot.

But he realised that that would not do.

Those beasts would be coming back for it when they

were ready to start up the river. If they found Bunter engaged in demolishing the contents, they were quite likely to get engaged in demolishing Bunter.

The fat junior lifted the parcel from the table.

"Oh crikey!" he gasped.

It was heavy!

It was, in fact, very heavy indeed!

Judging by its weight, Bob Cherry had packed huge supplies of foodstuffs in that parcel.

He heaved it to the door, and carried it out into the Remove passage. He bore it along to his own study—No. 7. Bunter's idea was to lock himself in that study and then get busy on the parcel.

Unluckily his study-mate, Peter Todd, was in Study No. 7. Peter stared at the fat Owl of the Remove and his burden.

"Hallo! What have you got there?" he asked.

"Oh, nothing!" gasped Bunter.

And he rolled on up the passage with his plunder, leaving Toddy staring.

At the end of the Remove passage were the box-room stairs. The fat junior clambered up the stairs, gasping under the weight of the big parcel.

He rolled breathless into the box-room at the top, shut the door, and turned the key.

All was safe now.

Harry Wharton & Co. could come back to Study No. 1 for that parcel as soon as they liked. They could hunt for it if they liked, and as long as they jolly well liked.

Having dumped down the parcel on the lid of Lord Mauleverer's big trunk, the fat junior fumbled for his penknife, and sawed through the string.

Then he unwrapped the sheets of brown paper.

His eyes glistened in anticipation behind his big spectacles. Already, in his mind's eye, Bunter beheld stacks of cakes, jam tarts, cream puffs, cheese cakes, bottles of ginger-beer—all sorts and conditions of good things.

It was a glorious vision—in his mind's eye. But it was not, alas! to be seen by any other eye.

The wrappings removed, a large cardboard box was revealed. Bunter jerked off the lid.

Within were a number of objects wrapped in old newspapers.

Why Bob Cherry should have wrapped up tuck in old newspapers was rather a mystery. But the mystery was soon revealed. Bob hadn't.

Unrolling the first that came to hand, Billy Bunter was astonished, if not delighted, by the sight of a brick.

He stared at it blankly.

Why Bob had packed a brick in a picnic parcel was an absolute puzzle. Bunter hurled it aside, and unrolled the next item. That also proved to be a brick.

"What the thump!" gasped the astonished Owl. "Is the silly ass potty, or what? What the dickens was he going to do with bricks at a picnic?"

He grabbed another item and unwrapped the newspaper. His little round eyes almost bulged through his big, round spectacles at the sight of a third brick. It was really amazing. Bob, it seemed, had gone round collecting bricks for a picnic.

The fat Owl grabbed packet after packet and unwrapped them. They did not all contain bricks. One contained an ancient boot; another a disused potato; a third, several empty sardine tins. Nothing of an edible nature came to light. Billy Bunter could eat almost anything; but even Bunter drew the line at bricks, old boots, mouldy potatoes, and sardine tins.

"Beast!" hissed Bunter.

He stood glaring at that precious parcel with a glare that might have cracked his spectacles.

The dreadful truth dawned on his fat brain.

Those beasts—those awful beasts—had jolly well known that he was listening outside Study No. 1.

They had fixed up this dud parcel, and left it for him to snaffle!

And while he was thus engaged, they were clearing off for Popper's Island in their boat—leaving Bunter behind!

No wonder they had chortled as they went!

This was the sort of thing that the beasts considered a joke!

"Oh, crikey!" gasped Bunter.

He had lost his interest in that parcel. Leaving string and wrappings, and old newspapers, bricks, and sardine-tins strewn about the box-room, Billy Bunter rolled hurriedly down the stairs again—scuttled breathlessly along the Remove passage, and fairly bolted out of the House. He headed for the boathouse as fast as his fat little legs could go. But he had a feeling that he would be too late!

And he was!

Seven smiling faces looked merry and bright in the roomy old boat that pulled up the shining Sark.

It was a glorious June afternoon.

There were plenty of Greyfriars' fellows on the river, on the landing-raft, and on the towpath; and all of them looked cheerful. But the merriest and brightest were the party in the Remove boat.

Wharton and Bob Cherry, Johnny Bull, and Nugent, pulled at the oars. Hurree Jamset Ram Singh sat in the bows. In the stern sat Marjorie Hazeldene and Clara Trevlyn, of Cliff House School. Fellows in other boats cast envious glances at the Famous Five and their pretty passengers.

Looking back, Bob Cherry, as he pulled, grinned over his oar at a fat figure that appeared on the raft by the boathouse.

It was small in the distance, but recognisable.

It was brandishing a fat fist after the boat—and probably shouting, but if so, the distance was too great for William George Bunter's dulcet tones to carry.

In the boat reposed a picnic-basket. It had been placed there before Bob Cherry conveyed the dud parcel to Study No. 1 in the Remove for the special behoof of Billy Bunter.

Now they were well on their way up the river—minus Bunter! It was going to be a gorgeous afternoon. Pulling up the shining river, in the summer sunshine, under a

9

blue sky dotted with fleecy clouds, was a sheer pleasure. And there was going to be a picnic on Popper's Island —rather regardless of the fact that that island was out of bounds.

Sir Hilton Popper, of Popper Court, was quite fierce on the subject of camping on the island. But, important gentleman as Sir Hilton was, the cheery chums of the Remove had actually forgotten him!

It would have surprised the lord of Popper Court could he have known, and realised, that his important existence could be forgotten! But there it was—the thoughtless schoolboys had given no more thought to Sir Hilton Popper, baronet, than to the gnats that buzzed in the summer sunshine.

"Hallo, hallo, hallo, that's jolly old Coker!" remarked Bob Cherry, when the Remove boat was about a mile up the Sark.

Sounds like a thrashing whale reached the ears of the Remove party. They could have guessed without looking that Coker of the Fifth was at hand. When Coker of the Fifth was rowing he always seemed to be earnestly intent on digging up the river.

Smiling faces glanced round at the Fifth Form boat. Greene was steering it, Coker and Potter were pulling. Potter, at least, was pulling—Coker was catching a marvellous succession of crabs. He was putting his beef into it, and his rugged face was red with effort; but the progress of the boat did not correspond with Coker's efforts. It crawled.

"What'll you give for a tow, Coker?" called out Bob, as the junior boat glided by.

Coker stared round.

"You cheeky young scoundrel——" he bawled. Then, catching sight of the Cliff House girls in the boat, Coker checked his eloquence.

"Race you, Coker!" chortled Johnny Bull.

"The racefulness would be terrific!" chuckled Hurree Jamset Ram Singh.

"For goodness' sake, Coker, let Greene take that oar!"

10

"Yarooh!" yelled Potter, as Coker's oar caught him a crack on the head

muttered Potter of the Fifth. "We don't want to be passed by every crew of cheeky fags on the river."

"Greene can't row, any more than you can, George Potter!" retorted Coker. "Why don't you pull? We're simply crawling."

"Leave off pulling, then, and we shall get on quicker."

Harry Wharton & Co. pulled on, leaving the Fifth Form boat floundering behind. The next bend of the Sark hid it from sight.

At that distance from the school the Famous Five had the Sark to themselves. Ahead of them rose the green mass of the island in the river. They pulled for the channel between the island and the Popper Court bank.

"Is that Sir Hilton Popper?" asked Marjorie Hazeldene, glancing at a tall, angular figure on the towpath.

"Oh!" ejaculated Harry Wharton.

He glanced round at the towpath. The angular old gentleman in riding-clothes, with a whip under his arm, was staring at the boat with bent brows over a gleaming eyeglass.

"Old Popper!" exclaimed Nugent.

"The esteemed and ridiculous Popper!"

"What rotten luck!"

"What does it matter?" asked Miss Clara.

"Um! Well it does, rather," said Harry. "Old Popper kicks up a fearful row if anyone lands on the island. He fancies it's his."

"Like his cheek!" remarked Miss Clara.

"But isn't it his?" asked Marjorie.

"Well, he says so, and nobody seems keen on going to law with him about it!" said Harry Wharton. "But everybody else says it's public land."

He glanced doubtfully at his comrades.

"The trouble is that the Head's put the island out of bounds, to stop bickering about it," he went on, "and old Popper, being a governor of the school, it's rather awkward. Perhaps—hem—per——"

"No perhaps about it," said Bob.

Grimmer and grimmer grew the frowning brow of

the lord of Popper Court as the Remove boat drew nearer. Sir Hilton had not the slightest doubt that he had spotted a picnic party bound for his island—as, indeed, he had!

Sir Hilton slipped his riding-whip down into his hand and waved it to the schoolboys in the boat.

"Here, you!" he called out.

"There, you!" called back Bob Cherry cheerily.

"What—what?" ejaculated Sir Hilton.

"Which—which!" answered Bob in the same cheerful tone. And the boat's crew chuckled.

They had certainly intended to land on Popper's Island. But they had not landed on it yet, so that was all right! Sir Hilton, so far, had nothing to report to the headmaster of Greyfriars. So Bob saw no reason for not exchanging a little light bandinage with the irascible old gentleman.

"What!" exclaimed Sir Hilton. "Boy! You are impertinent!"

"Man!" retorted Bob. "Same to you, and many of them!"

"Ha, ha, ha!"

"By gad," exclaimed Sir Hilton, "if I were near enough, you impudent young rascal, I would lay my riding-whip round you!"

"Jump!" suggested Bob.

"Ha, ha, ha!" roared the juniors, and Marjorie and Clara smiled.

Sir Hilton's face was quite purple. He came to the very edge of the bank, his eye gleaming through his eye-glass, gripping the riding-whip. It was clear what he would have done with that whip had Bob Cherry been within reach of it. Fortunately, Bob wasn't.

"Pull round the dashed old island," said Harry, laughing. "We can't picnic there now, that's a cert!"

"Better not!" agreed Johnny Bull.

"Much better, I think," said Marjorie, smiling. "Sir Hilton looks quite cross."

"He does—a few!" chuckled Nugent.

The boat pulled on. Sir Hilton Popper followed, along

the towpath, his fiery eye on the juniors. Evidently he suspected them of intending to land on that island, and he was not going to lose sight of them.

Having passed the island, the juniors pulled round to the other side, and turned back down the current. The wooded mass of the island hid the boat from the baronet's fiery eye.

"It's all right," remarked Harry Wharton. "We'll pull to that backwater we passed a quarter of a mile down; it's a lovely spot for camping, and no Poppers about!"

"Good egg!" agreed Bob.

The boat floated down on the current. The island hid Sir Hilton from the juniors, as it hid the juniors from Sir Hilton. But they heard his powerful voice ringing across the river:

"Joyce! Where are you, Joyce? Joyce! Where is that man? By gad, I will discharge him—— Oh, you are here! Joyce, a boat has gone round the island, under my very eyes! They are landing on the other side! They must be turned off immediately!"

"Yes, Sir Hilton! But——"

"Do not argue with me, Joyce! You will fetch a boat immediately, and I will cross to the island with you, and——"

"But——"

"Why are you standing there arguing, Joyce? Why do you not carry out my orders? Go at once!" thundered Sir Hilton.

"But, sir, is that the boat?" gasped the keeper.

"Eh! What! Oh, gad!"

The Remove boat glided into view again, past the lower end of the island. Sir Hilton glared at it. Joyce suppressed a grin.

"Oh!" gasped Sir Hilton.

He realised that the schoolboys had not landed on the other side of the island. They had simply circumnavigated it, and were going back down the river.

Seven smiling faces were turned towards the baronet on the towpath.

Bob Cherry waved his hand in farewell.

"Good-bye, Bluebell!" he called out.

"Ha, ha, ha!"

"You may go! Pah!"

Sir Hilton turned and stalked along the towpath; and Joyce did not grin again till his lordly back was turned.

As the boat pulled down the Sark, the angular figure of the lord of Popper Court stalked it, along the bank. Sir Hilton was still suspicious of the intentions of the picnickers.

But the chums of the Remove had quite given up the idea of camping on the island that afternoon. For Sir Hilton, great gun as he was, they did not care two straws; but they did not want a row with the Head when they got back to the school.

For a quarter of a mile the Remove boat pulled down the Sark, and then turned into a shady little backwater on the opposite side of the river, and disappeared from Sir Hilton's sight.

Quite indifferent to Sir Hilton, the chums of the Remove punted the boat up the shady backwater, to camp for the picnic on the bank, under a shady oak-tree.

And it was a happy picnic; really quite as good as camping on Popper's Island, with the additional advantage that there were no Poppers about!

Off and On!

"I SAY, you fellows!" yelled Billy Bunter.

More than an hour later, the fat figure of the Owl of the Remove stood on the towpath, opposite Popper's Island—on the very spot where Sir Hilton had stood.

The spot was deserted now, save for the fat Owl!

Billy Bunter stood there, dusty, fatigued, and perspiring, and hailed the island with his loudest squeak.

Having been left behind by the Remove boat, Bunter had walked. Walking in itself had no appeal for Bunter; but a picnic had—and rather than miss the picnic, Bunter had walked.

Standing on the bank, wiping a fat, perspiring face with his handkerchief, the Owl of the Remove hailed the picnickers on the island—not having the faintest or remotest idea that nobody was there!

Bunter knew that the picnic had been planned for Popper's Island. He had heard it discussed and settled. He had seen the chums of the Remove start up the river in the boat, with the Cliff House girls. So how was he to doubt that they had arrived at the island, and landed there according to plan?

He did not think of doubting it. They were there, of course—camping and picnicking in the shade of the old trees, hidden by bushes and foliage from view. The fact that he received no answer to his hail did not enlighten him. He was aware exactly how anxious the juniors were to see him! It was like the beasts to keep doggo, and pretend that they didn't hear a fellow!

"Wharton!" yelled Bunter.

Certainly his fat voice reached the island, and carried beyond it. If they were there, they must hear. And he was certain they were there.

"Bob Cherry, you beast!" roared Bunter.

They had had plenty of time to pull up to the island. Bunter, indeed, could have followed along the bank, keeping the boat in sight, had he been a little more active and a little less of a heavyweight. They had reached the island long ago, and that was certain to Bunter. That they had turned back after reaching it, and were now camped across the river a quarter of a mile down, he had no means of guessing.

His voice echoed; but there was no other answer. The

fat Owl shook a fat fist at the greenery on the island—
greenery which, he was convinced, hid a grinning party
of picnickers.

"Nugent, you rotter!" howled Bunter.

But answer there came none!

He fanned off flies with his handkerchief, dabbed
streaming perspiration from his fat face, and breathed
wrath.

"Beasts!" he howled.

They could hear him—of course they could. They
weren't going to fetch him across, chiefly because the Cliff
House girls were present, and they were jealous of Bunter's
good looks! Which was really unnecessary, for Bunter
was not thinking of Marjorie or Clara, charming as they
were; he was thinking of the tuck!

"I say, you fellows!" yelled Bunter. "I jolly well know
you're on that island! I say, if old Popper's about, he
will hear me, and you'll get into a row."

Bunter fancied that that would make them sit up and
take notice.

No doubt it would have done so had they been on
Popper's Island. Certainly they would not have wanted
the attention of Sir Hilton or his keepers drawn to the
fact that they were there.

"Do you hear?" yelled Bunter. "I say, you fellows! I
say, Wharton, I've got a message for you from Wingate of
the Sixth!"

No answer.

"I say, you fellows! Quelch is coming up the bank; he
jolly well knows you're there!"

Still there was no answer—no sign from the island.
Bunter gasped for breath, leaned on a tree by the towpath, and blinked across at the island through his big
spectacles, in speechless wrath.

If they did not come off in the boat for him, Bunter
was done! And it was getting clear that they weren't going
to! Apparently they were sitting tight, at the risk of
Bunter's yells bringing keepers to the spot.

"I say, Marjorie!" howled Bunter. "I say, tell those

beasts to bring the boat across. I've got a message from your brother."

Bunter paused, like Brutus, for a reply. But he had no better luck than Brutus! There was no reply.

"Marjorie, old dear!" squeaked Bunter. "I say, I'm here, you know! I say, your brother's fallen down the Remove staircase and broken his leg."

That Marjorie could hear, unmoved, the news that her brother, Hazel of the Remove, had fallen down the stairs and broken his leg, seemed improbable. Billy Bunter could not doubt that he would get an answer this time.

But no answer came!

Any other fellow, probably, would have given it up at that point. If the picnickers were on the island, it was plain that they did not want Bunter there. Some fellows would have been a little coy about barging in where they were not wanted.

Not so Bunter! Bunter was not particular about a hospitable welcome. What he was anxious about was the feed.

If he could, by hook or by crook, land himself on the picnickers, it was all right! They could not kick a fellow out, with girls present. Short of being kicked out, Bunter did not mind what his reception was like.

From up the river, in the direction of Courtfield Bridge, a boat glided into sight.

Billy Bunter fixed his eyes, and his spectacles, on it.

As it came nearer he gave a grunt of annoyance. He recognised three Fifth Form fellows in the boat—Coker and Potter and Greene.

Coker of the Fifth was the last fellow at Greyfriars to take the trouble to give a fag a lift.

Not that Coker was not a good-natured fellow. He was! But Coker was of the Fifth Form, Fifth Formy, so to speak. He would have regarded such a request as cheek. And Coker was not the man to stand anything in the nature of cheek from juniors.

As the Fifth Form boat came nearer, matters did not look promising for asking favours. All three of the seniors looked cross and annoyed.

Coker, clearly, was in a bad temper. Potter and Greene had goaded looks. Generally they were tactful with Horace Coker. But Coker's series of crab-catching exploits going up the river had tried their tempers sorely, especially as he had splashed them both from head to foot with water, at the same time telling them, with biting scorn, what clumsy duffers they were, and advising them to leave boats alone, and stick to a tub on a pond.

There had been argument in Coker's boat—warm argument. The idea had been to pull up to Courtfield Bridge, and thence walk to the bunshop for tea. But at the rate at which Coker's boat progressed, it looked as if they would reach the bridge about the time they were due at Greyfriars for calling-over. Giving up all hope of tea at the bunshop, Potter and Greene recklessly told Coker what they thought of his rowing, and of him personally; and Coker declared that he was jolly well fed-up with them, and would jolly well turn back—which Coker jolly well did!

Thus it was that Coker's boat came floating down the river past Popper's Island, in time to give Billy Bunter a lift—if Coker was so disposed!

As it slid into the channel between the island and the bank, Billy Bunter hailed it.

"I say, you fellows!"

Coker gave him a glare.

"I say, give me a lift across to the island, you fellows!" squeaked Bunter. "I say, my friends are picnicking there, and I'm late. I say, you might give a chap a lift across. I can't make Wharton hear!"

"Go and eat coke, you fat frog!" growled Potter.

"Shut up, you young ass!" snapped Greene.

That did it!

Coker, already glaring at Bunter, had been about to bark at him. Potter and Greene spoke first—which was enough for Coker! Automatically, as it were, Coker took the opposite view.

Instead of barking at Bunter, he barked at Potter and Greene.

"No need to bite the kid's head off!" he snapped. "Why shouldn't we give him a lift across?"

"Oh, rot!" grunted Potter.

"Rubbish!" grunted Greene.

That was more than enough for Coker! Opposition had its inevitable effect on the great Horace.

"Well, you can call it rot and rubbish if you like," he said, "but I believe in being good-natured! We're giving that kid a lift, see?"

"Look here——"

"You've wasted most of the afternoon already, Greene. A few minutes more won't hurt! Don't be a rotter!"

Potter and Greene suppressed their feelings. The Fifth Form boat pulled in to the bank.

"Hop in, Bunter!" said Coker.

Bunter thankfully hopped in.

"Thanks, old chap!" he gasped.

"Do you want a thick ear?" asked Coker unpleasantly. "If you do, you've only got to call me 'old chap' again."

Bunter did not want a thick ear! Judiciously he remained silent, while the seniors ferried him across to the island. He jumped ashore at the landing-place, and Potter pushed off again.

"You fathead! You've splashed me again!"

"Shut up, Potter!"

"Did we come out for a row or a bathe?"

"Stop jawing, Greene, for goodness' sake!"

Voices and splashing died away down the river. Coker & Co., and their boat, were gone. Billy Bunter, safely landed on Popper's Island at last, plunged through the trees and the underwoods, towards the glade in the middle of the island, where he expected to find the picnickers camped.

He reached the glade.

He found it empty.

The fat Owl blinked round him through his big spectacles.

"I say, you fellows!" he squeaked.

Silence!

"Beasts!" roared Bunter. "I know you're here! Dodging a fellow! I say, you rotters!"

Dead silence!

Bunter's first impression was that the picnickers knew that he had arrived, and had dodged him in the trees. But there was no sign of a picnic having been going on in the glade. For the first time, a dismaying doubt smote him. They were there—he was sure they were there! But it looked as if they weren't!

He was alone on Popper's Island!

"Oh, crikey!" repeated Bunter.

The picnickers were not, after all, there! There was no spread for Bunter! More serious still, if possible, there was no boat to take him off the island again.

He plunged back through the thickets to the water's edge. But it was futile to blink along the river for Coker's boat. Coker's boat was far out of sight by that time.

"Oh, lor'!" gasped Bunter.

All that afternoon he had been anxious to get on Popper's Island. Now he was on it, and only anxious to get off!

It had been difficult to get on! It was impossible to get off!

Bunter was stranded!

Missing!

"BUNTER!"

"Adsum!" answered Bob Cherry.

Wiggins was engaged in calling the roll.

Harry Wharton & Co. had returned, after the picnic,

in good time for calling-over. They were in their places with the Remove, in Hall, when Mr. Wiggins, the master of the Third, came in to call the names.

One member of the Remove was not there. That member of the Form was, in his own fat estimation, the most important member—being no other than William George Bunter.

In the estimation of other Removites, however, Billy Bunter's unimportance was unlimited—and plenty of fellows did not even notice that he was not there!

It was when Wiggins called his name that Bob became aware that Bunter was absent.

Without stopping to think, Bob answered for him.

It was not uncommon for a fellow to be late for calling-over, on a fine half-holiday. Neither was it uncommon for a good-natured fellow to keep him out of a row by answering to his name—if that little trick could be played successfully.

Bob, certainly, was a little thoughtless. Schoolboys often are. The happy, youthful mind does not always realise that there are good and solid reasons behind the rules laid down in a school.

Roll-call was not, as the juniors often considered it, merely a worry. It had its reasons and its uses.

It was a hundred to one that a fellow who cut roll was merely late. But there was always the odd chance that something might have happened to him.

Having answered for Bunter, and saved him, as he supposed, from a row, Bob dismissed the trifling matter from his mind.

After roll-call, he was thinking of anything but Bunter. There was boxing in the Rag to while away the time till prep. Bob Cherry and Johnny Bull had the gloves on with Vernon-Smith and Tom Redwing. Nobody was likely to remember Bunter.

Calling-over established—or was supposed to establish —the fact that a fellow who answered to his name was in the House. Bunter's name having been answered, Bunter was—officially—in the House—and that was that!

When the Remove went to the studies for prep, only two fellows noticed that Bunter did not turn up. They were Peter Todd and Tom Dutton, his study-mates in Study No. 7.

But they did not give that fact much heed. Bunter was unpunctuality itself. He loathed prep. He was quite likely to keep away from his study, unless a prefect spotted him.

Even Bunter, however, seldom or never cut prep entirely, as he did on this particular evening. Prep over, Peter wondered where the fat Owl was, and what he fancied he was up to. So he walked along to Study No. 1, and looked in on Wharton and Nugent.

"Seen a fat owl blithering about?" he asked.

"Bunter?" asked Harry. "Isn't he in your study?"

"He hasn't turned up for prep."

"The silly ass!" commented Nugent.

"I haven't seen anything of him this evening," said Peter. "I suppose he came in for roll."

"Must have," answered the captain of the Remove. "He would have been missed before this, if he hadn't."

"You were on a picnic this afternoon," remarked Peter. "Wasn't Bunter with you?"

Wharton and Nugent chuckled.

"No; we dodged him."

Thus it came to pass that it was not till bed-time for the Remove that Billy Bunter was missed. Wingate of the Sixth had the duty of shepherding the Remove to the dormitory; and then the fact transpired that Bunter was absent.

"Where's Bunter?" Wingate inquired.

Nobody knew.

"Go and look for him, Wharton!" said the prefect, frowning.

The head boy of the Remove went to look for Bunter.

The rest of the Remove were in bed in their dormitory, and Wingate waiting impatiently to switch off the light, when Harry Wharton arrived there—without Bunter.

"Can't find him, Wingate," said Harry.

"You can't find Bunter!" exclaimed Wingate.

"No; I've rooted all over the place."

"He's in the House, I suppose!" grunted the Greyfriars captain.

"I suppose so—he must have answered at roll. But I can't find him anywhere."

Wingate gave a grunt.

"Turn in!"

Wharton turned in, and Wingate switched off the light and went down to report to Mr. Quelch that one of his Form had failed to turn up at dorm.

Bob Cherry sat up in bed.

"Hasn't that blithering idiot come in?" he asked.

"Must have come in," answered Harry Wharton. "They'd have been after him long ago, if he hadn't answered at roll."

"Oh, crikey!" said Bob in dismay.

There was a chuckle from Hazeldene's bed.

"Didn't you answer for him at roll, Cherry?" he asked. "I thought you did."

"I jolly well did!" said Bob.

"You did!" exclaimed Wharton.

"Yes! I thought the silly ass was coming in late, and——"

"Oh, my hat! Then he may not have come in at all."

"We saw him on the raft this afternoon," said Nugent. "That was before four o'clock. Anybody seen him since?"

Nobody had seen him! Not a fellow in the Remove had the faintest idea where Billy Bunter might have spent his half-holiday.

It was five or six hours since he had been seen. He had not come in. Clearly, he could not be staying out of gates after bed-time of his own accord! Something had happened to Bunter!

"Dash it all!" said Johnny Bull. "It's rather a rotten idea to answer for another fellow at roll, when you come to think of it."

"Fat lot of good thinking of that now!" grunted Bob.

Rather late in the day, Bob realised those good, solid

reasons that lay behind the rules laid down by the school authorities.

Bunter was missing, and that unthinking, good-natured act had prevented him from being looked for till after darkness had fallen.

"Quelch will have to know," said Harry. "It's rotten luck, Bob, old man, but Quelchy's got to know."

"I know that!"

Bob was already slipping out of bed. It was not pleasant to face his Form-master with a statement of the facts. But, obviously, the Remove-master had to know that a member of his Form had not returned to the school. Already fellows were wondering whether the short-sighted Owl might have been run over by a car.

Mr. Quelch's door stood open. Wingate of the Sixth was there, and the Remove master was speaking to him.

"I can hardly understand this, Wingate. I was not present at calling-over, but Bunter must have answered to his name, or I should have been informed."

"That is so, sir," said Wingate. "But——" He stared round as a half-dressed junior appeared in the doorway.

Form-master and prefect stared at Bob Cherry. Bob's face was crimson. A glint came into Mr. Quelch's eyes.

"What does this mean, Cherry?" he snapped. "Why are you out of your dormitory?"

"About Bunter, sir," stammered Bob.

"Oh!" Mr. Quelch's frowning brow cleared. "If you are able to give me any information regarding Bunter——"

"He never came in, sir."

"He was present at calling-over, Cherry," said Wingate.

"He—he wasn't," stammered Bob.

"Nonsense!" rapped Mr. Quelch. "If any boy in my Form had failed to answer to his name, Mr. Wiggins would have informed me immediately."

"I—I—I answered, sir."

"What!"

"I—I answered for Bunter, sir!" gulped Bob.

Mr. Quelch looked at him. Handing out an "adsum" for a fellow late for roll, was regarded as quite a trifling matter by thoughtless schoolboys. Mr. Quelch's expression indicated that he did not regard it as a trifling matter, however. And, indeed, it was not, as was now only too clear to Bob Cherry.

"You answered for Bunter!" repeated Mr. Quelch enunciating each word with terrifying distinctness.

"Yes, sir!" gasped Bob. "I—I just thought he was late, sir, and—and——" His voice trailed off.

Mr. Quelch compressed his lips like a vice.

"Then Bunter was not present at roll-call?" he exclaimed.

"N-n-no, sir!"

"Do you know where he is?"

"No, sir."

"Something must have happened to the boy," said Mr. Quelch. "If there has been a serious accident, you have very much to answer for, Cherry."

"I—I know, sir!" groaned Bob. "I—I'm sorry."

"No doubt," said Mr. Quelch dryly. "Unfortunately your regret cannot undo the harm you have done. You may return to your dormitory, Cherry, I will deal with you in the morning. Wingate, search must be made immediately for Bunter. I will ring up the police station and ascertain whether anything is known of an accident. You may go, Cherry."

Bob Cherry went.

"Licked?" asked half a dozen voices, as he came back to the Remove dormitory.

"I'm getting that in the morning," answered Bob. "What on earth can have become of that fat ass?"

"Walked into a car," suggested Skinner.

"Oh, shut up, Skinner!" said two or three fellows.

Bob Cherry turned in—but not to sleep. For quite a long time there was a buzz of voices in the Remove dormitory. Fellows dropped off to sleep, one by one; but midnight had sounded before Bob's eyes closed. And the missing Owl had not returned.

"Oh, lor'!" groaned Billy Bunter.

It was uncommon—very uncommon indeed—for the fat Owl of the Remove to be awake at midnight.

But at midnight's stilly hour Billy Bunter was awake—wide awake—very wide awake indeed.

How long he had been on that beastly island Bunter hardly knew, but he knew that it seemed like centuries.

He was sleepy, but he could not sleep. He was hungry—fearfully hungry! It was a night of horror to Bunter.

At first the fat Owl had hoped to see some craft pass on the river, and get a lift off the island. Unfortunately Coker's boat was the last craft that passed.

It was not till the summer dusk was falling that Bunter resorted to the desperate expedient of shouting for help. If his shout reached any ears, those ears were most likely to belong to one of Sir Hilton Popper's keepers—and that meant a row at the school for having trespassed on Popper's Island.

But desperation at last drove Bunter to take that risk. But he took it in vain. No one appeared on the towpath—no figure in velveteens emerged from the shadowy woods along the Sark.

Darkness fell.

He was stranded for the night!

He had to realise it.

By that time the Remove were in bed. Evidently no one had any idea where Bunter was. It had not even occurred to the Famous Five that the fat Owl had contrived to land himself on Popper's Island, in the belief that they were there.

Coker & Co., certainly, might remember that they had ferried him across. But as he had told them that his friends were there they would hardly guess that he was stranded on the island without a boat.

Certainly no man in the Fifth was likely to notice whether a junior answered his name at roll or not. Not unless Bunter was inquired for up and down the school would Coker & Co. recall him to mind.

It meant an awful row if a boat had to be sent for

him to take him off a spot out of school bounds. But that was better than a night on the island.

It was an unpleasant alternative—but unpleasant as it was, it was not available. For, owing to Bob's hapless intervention, Bunter was not missed till bed-time, and Coker & Co. knew nothing of it.

Bunter's hope faded away as the summer night grew older.

Luckily it was a fine warm night—a lovely night in June. That was all right, so far as it went. But Bunter was sleepy, hungry, and growing very nervous.

Absolute solitude spelled safety, but there was something terrifying in it, all the same, and in the thickening, darkening shadows.

Bunter had long ceased to shout. If nobody had heard him before darkness fell, nobody was likely to hear him at a later hour.

Moreover, at a late hour of the night, unpleasant characters might be abroad—rough poachers in the Popper Court Woods; tramps camping out along the river. Bunter longed to see a human face—but not that of a poacher or a tramp.

He groaned.

Almost any fellow in the Greyfriars Remove, excepting Bunter, would have risked a swim across the channel to the towpath. The distance was not great.

Bunter did not even think of it.

Any fellow who had asked Bunter whether he could swim, would have been told that he was the best swimmer in the Remove, if not in the whole school. But at the bottom of his fat heart Billy Bunter had a misgiving about his swimming powers. He would have stated that he could swim like a duck. But once in the water he had reason to fear that his exploits would rather resemble those of a stone than a duck.

Anyhow he did not think of trying it on.

He thought of curling up in the thickets and trying to sleep. But he was too hungry and alarmed to sleep. In

28

fact, he hardly dared to blink into the dark circling shadows.

He sat down at last at the foot of a tree, among the willows at the edge of the island. Hungry and alarmed as he was, he was getting more and more sleepy, and he nodded a little. He was dozing dismally, when a sound from the silence of the woods reached him.

It was a distant shout.

The fat Owl started into wide wakefulness. Was it rescue at last? Had those beasts guessed where he was? Or had that ass Coker told what he knew? Someone, at all events, was at hand—and what could it mean but rescue?

Bunter's little round eyes gleamed through his big round spectacles. A caning from Quelch, even a whopping from the Head, meant little, if only he could get to supper and bed.

There was another shout, distinctly echoing. A light flashed in the darkness of the woods on the river bank, but there was no sign or sound of a boat on the river.

Bunter groaned dismally. It was not rescue; it was something going on in Popper Court Woods—most likely Sir Hilton's keepers after poachers.

Again came a shout, and then another and another. Several voices were calling from different quarters; they seemed to be coming from the direction of Popper Court, Sir Hilton's residence, a mile away across the wood.

"Beasts!" groaned Bunter.

But he had a glimpse of hope now. He was ready to face even the wrath of Sir Hilton Popper to get off that dreadful island. If any of the keepers came within call, Bunter was going to howl for help and chance it.

Across the channel, from the towpath, came a sound of rustling as someone hurriedly forced a way out of the thick wood. Bunter had a glimpse for a second of a figure that emerged on the towpath.

But he did not call out.

He blinked at that figure in terror.

It was not a keeper; it was a man who stood panting,

29

with bent head, listening; obviously a fugitive. And Bunter did not doubt that he was a poacher for whom the keepers were hunting.

Only for a few seconds the hunted man stood there, then there was a splash in the water.

The man was swimming the river.

Bunter leaned on the tree, blotted from sight in the darkness under it, his fat heart thumping. Till then the solitude had seemed awful; now the fat junior realised that solitude was infinitely preferable to a meeting in the dark with a lawless and desperate man.

He knew that the man was not swimming across the Sark; he was heading for the island. He heard the swift strokes as the swimmer cleft his way across the channel; he heard the splashing as he landed and the rustle of the willows as the man plunged among them.

His fat heart stood still.

He could not see the man in the blackness under the branches, neither could the man see him; but within a dozen feet of him a desperate man, dripping with water, crouched, and Bunter heard his panting breath. Another sound, strange enough, reached his fat ears—a clinking sound, as of metal. The man was carrying something— something that clinked like pots and pans in a bag. Bunter noticed the sound without heeding it.

Silence followed.

The panting breath was subdued; not a sound reached the Owl of the Remove. He could almost have fancied that it was a dream, and that he was still alone on the island in the river. But he knew—knew only too well— that the surrounding darkness hid a crouching, desperate man. The man was silent; and Billy Bunter was, if possible, still more silent. Not for worlds would he have made his presence known to that hunted skulker of the night.

Lights flashed in the dark wood again. Footsteps and voices sounded, and dim figures appeared in the moongleam on the towpath.

A Thief in the Night!

" JOYCE! "

"Sir Hilton——"

"You have missed him! "

"I think he came this way, sir! I——"

"You are mistaken! He did nothing of the kind! I am convinced that he was making off towards the common."

"I heard——"

"Nonsense! "

"I think——"

"Nonsense, Joyce! "

Billy Bunter heard every word across the narrow arm of the Sark. He could see the tall, angular figure of Sir Hilton Popper, and catch the gleam of the monocle in the baronet's eye.

Joyce, the keeper, stood silent. The autocrat of Popper Court was not a man to be argued with.

That they were in pursuit of the unknown man who had swum out to the island, Bunter knew. He could have called across the information they wanted. But he did not dare to utter a sound, with the hunted man crouching so near him in the gloom.

Bunter knew what they wanted to know—but Bunter, like Brer Fox, lay low and said "nuffin."

"He has escaped! " Sir Hilton's angry bark came clearly. "It was Leech; I saw him distinctly! It was Leech, Joyce! The man I discharged this morning for impertinence! It was Leech! You can swear to that, Joyce! "

"I only saw a shadder, sir——"

"You are a fool, Joyce! "

"Yes, Sir Hilton."

"No doubt he would have escaped unseen had I not awakened. My keepers, I have no doubt, would have

31

taken no notice of him and allowed him to escape with his plunder."   .

"As soon as I heard you call, sir——"

"Don't argue with me, Joyce! You have not done your duty! None of my keepers have done their duty! It was Leech—I am absolutely convinced that it was Leech! He knew his way about the house, of course. I saw him distinctly—at least, with sufficient distinctness. But if you had taken the trouble to keep your eyes open, Joyce, there would have been no doubt. He must have passed within a few yards of you when I followed him from the house——"

"I saw a shadder——"

"If you cannot swear to his identity, Joyce, you may as well hold your tongue! If you had followed in the right direction the rascal would have been in our hands by now!"

"I think——"

"Don't talk nonsense, Joyce! By this time he is half-way across Courtfield common with the Popper Court silver! Do you understand? Can you understand that I am put to a loss of more than £1,000 by your incapacity, Joyce?"

"I'm sure I heard him, sir——"

"Nonsense! If he escapes with his plunder, and cannot be unmistakably identified, he will snap his fingers at us."

"The police, sir——"

"I shall telephone to the police station the moment I return to the house. He shall be found—his lodgings in Courtfield searched—he shall be detained on suspicion, at least! The silver tankards he has purloined are heirlooms in my family; I am responsible for them. If you had not taken the wrong direction, Joyce, I should not have followed you here, and he would not have escaped."

"But, Sir Hilton——"

"You have wasted enough time already, Joyce; do not waste more in idle talk. Call the others and make for the common at once, while I return to the house and ring up the police——"

"But, sir——"

"Are you going to argue with me, Joyce, or carry out my orders?" barked Sir Hilton.

Joyce drew a deep breath.

"Very well, sir."

"Go at once! At once, I say! Why are you wasting time? I tell you that it was Leech—I am practically convinced that it was Leech—and he may yet be caught with the plunder on him."

"Yes, Sir Hilton."

Joyce went back into the wood; Sir Hilton Popper, fuming, stalked after him, and both disappeared from Billy Bunter's eyes.

Sir Hilton fancied that the man had broken out in the other direction, towards the open spaces of Courtfield common. And now Joyce was calling the other keepers to search in that direction. They were not likely to have much luck, as every step took them farther and farther away from the drenched man crouching on the island.

"Oh, lor'!" breathed Billy Bunter—not aloud.

He understood now that it was not a case of poaching. There had been a burglary at Popper Court, and the thief had had a narrow escape. And he was now crouching within a few yards of Billy Bunter—with his plunder! Bunter knew now the meaning of the clinking sound he had heard; it had been made by the celebrated Popper Court silver, packed in a bag in the grasp of the man who had stolen it.

Silent, Bunter strained his fat ears to listen.

Surely the man would go, now that the coast was clear! Bunter longed to hear him go. He trembled at the thought of the rascal discovering him there. What would the villain do if he spotted him?

But it was long before the unseen man stirred.

Not till the last sound had died away in the shadowy woods, and it was certain that no one was anywhere near at hand, did the crouching man move.

Was he going?

He could only get off the island by swimming, and

33

Bunter expected to hear a sound of a plunge in the water.

But that sound did not come.

The man was moving—he could hear him move! The willows swayed and rustled and brushed. Why did he not go?

But it was evident that Leech did not know that anyone was on the island with him. His pursuers were gone, and were far distant now, and certainly it was not likely to cross his mind that a fat schoolboy had been stranded on the island in the river. So long as Bunter kept silent in the dark, he was safe—and he kept very silent indeed.

At length, to the fat junior's intense relief, he heard a splashing sound. The man was going at last!

Bunter heard the water ripple from the strokes of a swimmer. Blinking out of the darkness under the branches, he spotted a head on the moonlit water.

Swift strokes carried the man to the bank. Bunter, with his spectacles glued on him, saw him drag himself from the river—a dim, half-seen figure in the moongleam.

Swiftly that shadowy figure darted across the towpath to the wood. During the next few minutes faint sounds were wafted to Bunter. The man was out of his sight, but still there, and the fat junior guessed that he was wringing the water out of his clothes before he went.

But all sound died away at last.

The man was gone!

Bunter breathed a deep, deep breath of thankfulness. He was solitary again; but, for the first time, he saw the charms that sages have seen in the face of solitude! The loneliness of the Sahara would have been preferable to such company!

"Oh, dear!" groaned Bunter. "Thank goodness that beast is gone, but—— Oh, dear! Oh, crikey!"

Faintly, afar across the woods, sounded a distant stroke, followed by another. It was two o'clock!

"Oh, lor'!" groaned Bunter.

He sat down again, and leaned on the tree. His fat head nodded over his fat chest. Even hunger was forgotten in overpowering drowsiness. At last Billy Bunter slept, and his deep snore made a more or less musical accompaniment to the ripple of the Sark.

"Out all night!"
"Great pip!"

In the Remove dormitory, when the rising-bell clanged out in the sunny morning, every fellow stared at Billy Bunter's empty bed.

That bed had not been slept in.

Bunter, evidently, had not returned overnight! The fat Owl of the Remove had had a night out!

It was the first time such a thing had happened, so far as any Remove fellow knew. Where was Bunter?

Bob Cherry's usually cheery face was deeply worried when he went down with his chums. He blamed himself for what he had done; though really it was only what thoughtless fellows had done dozens of times, with no harm coming of it. Nevertheless, but for that unlucky "adsum" in Hall the evening before, Bunter would have been looked for while the long summer day was still light. Clearly, if he had been looked for after dark, he had not been found.

Mr. Quelch was already out of the House when the Famous Five appeared in the quad. His face was very sombre, and he frowned grimly at the sight of Bob. His look did not invite questioning; but the juniors were anxious about the missing Owl, and they ventured.

"May we ask if Bunter has been found, sir?" asked Harry Wharton.

"He has not been found!" barked Mr. Quelch.

He gave Bob a very grim look.

"No one appears to know where the boy went yesterday afternoon," he said. "There is no trace of him to be found. If he is unharmed, it is inconceivable that he has not returned to the school. Had search been made earlier, doubtless something might have been learned."

Then, as he read the dismal dismay in Bob's unhappy face, the Remove master relented.

"You see now, Cherry, the harm that may be done by

35

a thoughtless infraction of the rules of the school!" he said. "I shall not punish you—I think you realise your fault sufficiently."

"Yes, sir!" mumbled Bob.

"I may add," said Mr. Quelch, "that I can learn nothing of any accident. Nothing is known at the police station or the Courtfield Hospital. Something must have happened to Bunter; but we must hope that it was not an accident of a serious nature."

He walked away to speak to Mr. Prout, who came puffing into the quad. When the bell rang for prayers, all the school knew that Bunter of the Remove was missing.

After prayers, some of the Sixth Form prefects went out, on foot or on bicycles. It seemed that there was going to be a hunt for Bunter, now that a new day had dawned.

When the Famous Five came out after breakfast, Coker of the Fifth came up to them in the quad. Coker, by that time, had heard, like the rest of the school, that Bunter of the Remove was missing, and had been missing all night.

Coker was frowning.

"What's all this about Bunter?" he demanded gruffly.

"He's missing!" said Harry.

"Well, from what I hear, he was missing all the afternoon yesterday," said Coker. "Why haven't you told your beak where he was?"

The Famous Five stared at Coker.

"Because we don't know, fathead!" said Bob.

"You were the last fellows who saw him—Wharton, at least," said Coker. "You're bound to tell your beak! If you get into a row for trespassing on Popper's Island, that can't be helped."

"What the thump are you talking about?" demanded Wharton. "We haven't been on Popper's Island for weeks!"

"Don't talk rot!" snapped Coker. "You were there yesterday afternoon, or Bunter wouldn't have said so."

"Did Bunter say so?"

"Yes, he did, when he asked me for a lift across to the

36

island!" grunted Coker. "He said his friends were picnicking there, and mentioned your name, Wharton, so you were there."

"Oh, my hat!" gasped the captain of the Remove.

He understood now.

"That howling ass!" exclaimed Nugent. "He fancied we were picnicking on Popper's Island!"

"And weren't you?" demanded Coker. "I saw you going up the river!"

"No, ass! We were going there, but old Popper turned up on the bank, and we went somewhere else!" growled Johnny Bull. "If that fat duffer fancied we were on the island——"

"Well, he jolly well did, or he wouldn't have asked for a lift across," said Coker. "I landed him there, I know that!"

"Oh, scissors!" gasped Bob. "Can he have been on the island all night? He would be too funky to swim off, if he was stranded there."

Coker whistled.

"Oh, you ass!" said Bob. "Why the thump did you give him a lift across? If we'd known that——"

"Don't be cheeky!" snapped Coker.

"We might have guessed he was after us, only we knew he was too jolly lazy to pull up the river!" said Harry. "I never thought of the fat ass walking it, and getting a lift across. Why the thump didn't you tell Quelch last night?"

"Why the thump should I, when I never knew till ten minutes ago that the young ass was missing?" snapped Coker. "I can't make out why he wasn't missed at calling-over!"

"Oh!" said Bob, reddening. It seemed as if he was never to hear the end of that unlucky "adsum."

"They ought to have missed him then, and inquired after him," said Coker. "I can't make out why they didn't. If I'd heard anything about it before the Fifth went to roost, of course I should have told Quelch."

"Oh, dear!" murmured Bob.

"Well, you'd better tell Quelch now," said Harry. "If you planted Bunter on Popper's Island, it's pretty certain that he's there now. He couldn't get off, unless a boat passed, and very likely one didn't."

Coker gave an angry grunt.

"I'm going to tell Quelch! I'll jolly well kick the young ass when he comes back, too! Bother him!"

And Coker stalked away. Mr. Quelch was in the quad, talking to Prout and Wiggins; the three masters discussing the mystery of the missing Owl.

Harry Wharton & Co. watched Coker of the Fifth, as he stalked up to the group. The mystery of Billy Bunter's absence was clear to them now; and it was going to be made clear to the masters. And as Popper's Island was strictly and severely out of school bounds, it looked as if there was going to be a "row."

The Vials of Wrath!

PROUT boomed.

Mr. Quelch compressed his lips; Mr. Wiggins shrugged his shoulders. But Mr. Prout boomed.

All the masters were, of course, relieved to hear that Bunter's whereabouts were known; that the fat junior was probably safe and sound, and no doubt little the worse for a night out in balmy June.

Mr. Quelch hurried away at once to direct the boat-keeper to take a boat up to Popper's Island and bring Bunter off, if he was there. Mr. Wiggins walked back to the House to spread the news. But Coker was not at liberty to depart, after handing out his valuable information. Coker had to stand where he was, and listen to his Form-master.

"I can scarcely believe," said Mr. Prout, fixing Coker, like the Ancient Mariner, with a glittering eye—"I can scarcely credit, Coker, that you—even you, the most obtuse boy in my Form—could be guilty of this act of thoughtless and disrespectful folly!"

Coker blinked at him.

He did not understand.

He was used, of course, to fault-finding from Prout. Prout always had some fault or other to find with him; even in such simple matters as spelling, as when, for instance, Coker spelt "occiput" with an x instead of a double c—which Coker knew was right if Prout didn't.

But for the life of him, Coker could not see what he had done amiss now. Here was Prout booming at him in the middle of the quad for nothing at all.

"But I had to tell Mr. Quelch, sir," stammered Coker. "He seems to be anxious about the young ass—I mean Bunter—so I thought I'd better tell him where he was."

"I am not alluding to that, Coker! Have you no sense?" boomed Prout. "I am glad, at least, that you have had the frankness to confess to your fault, considering the serious consequences to which it has led."

"My fault, sir?" gasped the bewildered Coker.

"Your most serious dereliction of duty!" boomed Prout. "Your unthinking and reckless disregard of authority, Coker!"

"What have I done, sir?" stuttered Coker.

"What have you done?" boomed Prout. "Have you not confessed that you landed a Remove boy yesterday on the island in the river belonging to Sir Hilton Popper?"

"Oh! Yes, sir!"

"Are you aware, or are you not aware, that that island is out of school bounds?" boomed Prout.

Coker started.

He was aware of it, of course. Everybody at Greyfriars was. But certainly he had not called it to mind when he gave Bunter that lift in his boat. His mind had been chiefly occupied at that time with pointing out to Potter and Greene what silly idiots they were.

"Are you aware, or are you not aware, that Sir Hilton Popper has threatened to prosecute any trespasser on that island?" resumed Prout.

"Oh!" gasped Coker. "Yes."

"Yet, knowing this, you helped a foolish junior boy to defy the prohibition of a landowner who is also a governor of this school!"

"Oh!" gasped Coker.

Coker had not thought of it in that light. He had not, in fact, thought at all. Thinking was not Coker's long suit.

He had given a kid a lift in his boat. That was all. But put as Prout put it, it was a much more serious matter than that.

"I am amazed," said Prout. "I am astonished. You, a senior boy in the Fifth Form—my Form! You have trespassed, or, at least, been a party to trespassing, on Sir Hilton Popper's property——"

"'Tain't his property, sir!" hooted the goaded Coker.

"What—what?"

"Everybody knows that that island's public land!" hooted Coker. "That old hunks——"

"Who—what——"

"Old Popper—has enclosed it, and makes out that it's his, but it jolly well isn't, and I'd jolly well tell him so to his face!" said Coker. "I'd land on that island right under his nose if it wasn't out of bounds!"

Prout gazed at Coker.

So did Harry Wharton & Co. and about thirty other fellows, drawn to the spot by Prout's boom.

"Old Coker's asking for it!" murmured the Bounder.

"The askfulness is terrific."

"He's right!" grunted Johnny Bull.

But Coker of the Fifth was seldom, if ever, judicious. He was, on the other hand, born to trouble as the sparks fly upward.

Prout, seemingly bereft of speech, gazed at him, his boom quite interrupted. Coker went on:

"Dr. Locke's put the island out of bounds, sir. I know that. But a lot of fellows think it's rotten!"

"What?" breathed Prout.

"I don't believe in giving in to a greedy old hunks!" said Coker. "I'm bound to obey my headmaster, but I wouldn't care a brass button for old Popper! If he talked to me, I'd tell him to go an eat coke fast enough!"

"You are speaking of a governor of the school, Coker!" gurgled Prout.

"I know, sir! I jolly well think——"

"Silence!" Prout recovered his breath and his boom. "Do not attempt to defend your conduct, Coker, by adding insolence to insolence! You will take five hundred lines!"

"Oh!" gasped Coker. "Look here, sir——"

"Another word, and I will make your imposition a thousand lines, Coker!" roared Mr. Prout.

Coker stood dumb.

Mr. Prout, pink with wrath, rolled away.

Horace Coker stood staring after him.

Potter and Greene, who had joined the crowd of on-lookers, exchanged a grin. It was not uncommon for Coker to argue with his Form-master. It did not make him popular with Prout, but it often afforded the Fifth Form a little entertainment.

"Well, you've got the old bean's rag out now, Coker!" remarked Potter—waiting till Prout was out of hearing before he made that remark.

"Five hundred lines!" gasped Coker.

"Lucky that's the lot!" remarked Green. "Prout looked like making it a whopping."

"Blow Prout!"

"But Prout——" gasped Greene.

"Prout likes to be asked to dinner at Popper Court!" hooted Coker. "That's what's the matter with Prout!"

"Ha, ha, ha!"

"For goodness' sake, shut up, Coker—if Prout heard you——"

"I don't care if he does! Five hundred lines! I never set foot on the putrid island, did I? But I jolly well will!"

"Coker, old man, for goodness' sake don't be a goat!" pleaded Potter. "Prout would be as mad as a hatter if——"

"Let him!" hooted Coker. "Let him make it a thousand lines if he likes! Let him make it two thousand! Let him make it all the Georgics that that silly ass, Virgil, ever wrote! I don't care! You'll see! I'm going up to the island after class! I'll show old Popper! I'll show old Prout!"

"Coker——"

"Old chap——"

"You'll see!" hooted Coker. "I'm going up to that island after class, and you fellows can come with me——"

"I'll watch it!" gasped Potter.

"I'll go alone if you're funky! I'm going! Who's old Popper?" demanded Coker, in a voice that would certainly have reached Prout's portly ears, had not that majestic gentleman, fortunately, gone into the House. "Who the thump is Sir Hilton Popper, Baronet? Everybody knows it was a dashed City alderman gave James I a thousand pounds for the title! They used to sell 'em like doughnuts——"

"Ha, ha, ha!"

"Let him come popping in when I'm on the island, that's all! I'll tell him what I think of him!" hooted Coker. "He doesn't ask me to dinner—as he does Prout——"

"Ha, ha, ha!"

"Coker, old man——"

"You'll see!" roared Coker. "You'll jolly well see! And I can jolly well say out plain—— Bother that beastly bell!"

"Ha, ha, ha!"

It was the bell for class. It cut short the flow of Horace Coker's eloquence. Coker went in with the Fifth, in a state of seething indignation. He did not find Prout pleasant in Form that morning.

"I say, you fellows!"

"Hallo, hallo, hallo! Here he is!"

"Here's Bunter!"

"So you've got back!" said Harry Wharton. "Did they pick you up on Popper's Island?"

"Yes! I say, you fellows, I've had a fearful time!" said Bunter. "I was awake all night—never closed my eyes, you know—not once! I haven't had any sleep! Of course, I can stand it—I'm pretty tough! I don't suppose you fellows could! I think you fellows might have come and got me off, though! That silly ass of a boatman woke me up by poking me with an oar——"

"Ha, ha, ha!"

"Blessed if I see anything to cackle at!" said Bunter warmly. "If you think it's funny to be stranded out all night, not sleeping a wink——"

"You weren't sleeping a wink when the boatkeeper woke you up?" asked Bob.

"Eh? No—yes—I—mean——"

"Ha, ha, ha!"

"What I mean is, I never slept a wink till—till I dropped off to sleep in——"

"Fellows often don't!" said Bob gravely.

"Ha, ha, ha!"

"Well, you can cackle!" said Bunter. "But I can tell you I've been through a fearful time, and it's all your fault! I thought you were on the island having that picnic! That idiot Coker ought to have told them where I was. Lucky I came through it alive——"

"I don't see the luck in that!" remarked Skinner.

"Beast!"

"Were you hungry?" grinned the Bounder.

"Frightfully! I never had any tea, you know, and no supper, and not even any brekker, till I got back here! Fancy that!"

"Lucky you've got enough fat to live on, like a polar bear!"

"Oh, really, Smithy——"

"I fancy Bunter's punished the grub since he got in!" chuckled Peter Todd.

"Well, I've had something to eat!" admitted Bunter. "I can tell you I needed it! Now I want some sleep! Not this moment, you know—but in third school. I think Quelch ought to let me sleep this morning, as I never had any sleep last night."

"Better not tell him that the boatkeeper woke you out of the sleep you never had, then!" suggested Skinner.

"Ha, ha, ha!"

"Oh, cackle!" said Bunter, disdainfully. "I should have expected my pals to be anxious about me, out at night, starving, and in fearful danger. But I suppose you were only thinking of yourselves—as usual!"

As a matter of fact, most of the Remove fellows had been thinking a good deal of the missing Owl, and feeling anxious about him. But now that he had turned up safe and sound, and none the worse for his night out, naturally their concern had evaporated.

"Quelch wasn't sympathetic," went on Bunter. "I thought he would be feeling it, you know. Instead of that, he's given me two hundred lines for going on that putrid island. That's his sort of sympathy!"

"Ha, ha, ha!"

"I shall expect you fellows to whack out those lines, as it's all your fault," said Bunter. "If you'd been on the island, it would have been all right. Leaving a fellow stranded all night——"

"How were we to know you were there, fathead?" asked Nugent.

"Now I've got lines for going on the island," said Bunter. "Lot Quelch cares about a fellow going through hunger and danger and——"

"We can guess you were hungry!" grinned Bob Cherry. "But where was the jolly old danger? I suppose you were in a blue funk, in the dark; but darkness doesn't bite."

"Suppose that burglar had spotted me——"

"That what?"

"Burglar!"

The juniors gazed at Bunter! This was the first they had heard of the burglar.

"What is the fat ass blithering about now?" asked Toddy. "Was there a burglary on Popper's Island? What did the burglar burgle?"

"Not on the island, fathead!" said Bunter. "At Popper Court, and the burglar swam off to the island, with old Popper and his keepers after him."

"Oh, my hat!"

"I wasn't scared, of course," said Bunter. "But I thought I'd better keep out of sight. I've no doubt he had a revolver! In fact, I saw it! But for that I should have collared him, and called out to old Popper."

"Yes—I can see you collaring burglars!" gasped Bob. "Just in your line! Did anyone get on the island while you were there?"

"Yes—that burglar!"

"Sure it wasn't a pirate landed from a lugger?" asked Bob.

"Ha, ha, ha!" yelled the Removites.

"You silly ass!" howled Bunter. "Of course it wasn't! It was a burglar—a big, savage, fierce-looking desperado. I couldn't see him in the dark——"

"Ha, ha, ha!"

"You'd better give his description to the police," gasped Smithy. "Only don't mention that you couldn't see him in the dark."

"Ha, ha, ha!"

"I mean, I had a glimpse of him—a fierce-looking ruffian," said Bunter, "I'd have tackled him fast enough, though, but for his knife——"

"His knife?"

"Yes, he had a knife—or, rather, a dagger—one of those long, flashing daggers you see on the films——"

"As well as a revolver?"

"Eh? No! Yes! I—I mean, a revolver! That is, he had a

45

knife as well as a revolver! One in each hand, you know."

"Oh, crumbs!"

"But for that, I'd have bagged the scoundrel and got old Popper's silver back," said Bunter. "I knew just where he was—hiding in that bunch of willows—though I couldn't see him."

"Oh! You couldn't see him?"

"Not after he got on the island. I spotted him swimming across from the bank," explained Bunter.

"Some swimmer!" grinned Bob. "Fancy a burglar swimming with a revolver in one hand and a knife in the other, you fellows! He must have had them while he was swimming, as Bunter only saw him in the water."

"Oh!" gasped Bunter. "I—I mean——"

"Yes, tell us what you mean," said Bob encouragingly. "I suppose you dreamed this before the boat-keeper woke you up?"

"Ha, ha, ha!"

"I didn't dream it!" yelled Bunter.

"Well, if you're making it up now, you ought to be able to make up a better one. You've had a lot of practice."

"If you fellows don't believe me——"

"Believe you!" gasped Bob. "You're not expecting anybody to believe you, are you?"

"It's true!" howled Bunter.

"Ha, ha, ha!"

"The believefulness is not terrific!" chuckled Hurree Jamset Ram Singh.

"I tell you the burglar came out swimming to the island in the middle of the night——"

"Go it!"

"He hid in the willows till old Popper was gone, and then swam off again——"

"Pile it on!"

"He had a bag of plunder, and I heard old Popper say it was the Popper Court silver, worth a thousand pounds——"

"Keep it up!"

46

"He said it was a man named Leech, whom he had sacked!" howled Bunter. "Old Popper gave him the sack——"

"And he carried off old Popper's silver in the sack?" asked Skinner.

"Ha, ha, ha!"

"Not that sack, you silly ass——"

"Ha, ha, ha!"

The bell for third school called the Remove back to their Form-room. Bunter, much to his annoyance, had to go in with the rest—Quelch apparently seeing no reason why the fat Owl should sleep through third school. The Remove were grinning as they went in.

Not a fellow in the Form believed in Bunter's burglar. Billy Bunter never could tell a plain, unvarnished tale; and the trimmings he added to it made it rather too incredible.

But though the revolver and the knife were figments of Bunter's fertile imagination, reminiscences of the wild and woolly western films he had seen, there really had been a burglar! Bunter knew that! And after third school he hooked Peter Todd by the arm when the Remove came out.

"I say, Toddy, about that burglar I——" he began.

"The one you dreamed of?" asked Peter.

"Fathead! That burglar on the island——"

"That's the one!" said Peter.

"You silly ass! Look here, do you think I'd better tell Quelch about it?"

Peter stared at him.

"Well, yes, if you want to be licked for trying to pull Quelch's leg," he answered. "If you want my advice, you'd better keep your film stunts for the Remove! They won't do for beaks."

"But it's true!" shrieked Bunter.

"Ha, ha, ha!"

"You—you—you sniggering idiot!" hooted Bunter. "Have you ever known me tell a lie?"

Peter almost fell down.

47

"Have I?" he stuttered. "Have I ever known you tell anything else?"

"Beast!"

Billy Bunter decided not to report his thrilling adventure to Mr. Quelch. Nobody in the Remove believed him, and he doubted whether Quelch would. And as William George Bunter was constitutionally incapable of keeping to the facts, it was very probable that Quelch wouldn't!

Startling News!

"HEARD?" asked Hobson of the Shell.

Hobby of the Shell had been down to Courtfield on his bike after dinner. He came back, put up his jigger, and walked into the quad, full of news.

"Burglars at Popper Court!" announced Hobby.

Which was enough to draw an interested crowd.

"Old Popper's place?" asked Bob Cherry.

"Yes—all the jolly old silver snaffled!" said Hobby. "Everybody in Courtfield is buzzing with it. They've got Inspector Grimes on the job. No end of excitement in the town."

"Well, my hat!" said Bob.

He remembered Bunter's burglar—hitherto dismissed as a figment of the fat Owl's imagination.

"Let's hear it, Hobby!" said a dozen voices.

Hobby was only too pleased to let them hear it. He was full of it. He had gone down to the sports shop at Courtfield about a new bat, but he had almost forgotten his new bat in the thrill of this startling news. Startling things did not happen very often round about Greyfriars.

"It happened last night," he said. "From what I hear, old Popper heard a noise, and went down, and spotted a burglar just jumping from a window, with loot in a bag. He got after him, with some of his keepers, and there was a chase in the woods."

"Did they get him?"

"No fear! He got clear," said Hobby. "But the police detained a man on suspicion, though they've let him go since. Man named Leech."

"Leech!" repeated Harry Wharton. Bunter had mentioned that name.

"This man Leech," went on Hobby, "was a manservant at Popper Court, and old Popper sacked him only yesterday or the day before. I don't know—quite lately, anyhow. He had done something or other——"

"Wanted his wages, perhaps?" suggested Skinner.

Some of the fellows chuckled. Sir Hilton Popper was not, perhaps, aware of it, but all the neighbourhood knew that his estate was covered by mortgages almost as thickly as by his old trees. At the Peal of Bells in Courtfield it was no secret that the wages of some of the household staff at the baronet's mansion were in arrear, and from that centre of local gossip such news trickled in all directions.

Probably it never occurred to the lofty lord of Popper Court that his menservants discussed him and his affairs at the Peal of Bells. But they undoubtedly did!

"Well, I don't know what the man did!" said Hobby, grinning. "Anyhow, old Popper sacked him, and he thinks that the man came back at night and snaffled his silver."

"Best chromium-plated, too!" said Skinner.

"Oh, that's rot!" said Bob. "The Popper silver is jolly well known—some of it is heirlooms, belonged to the family for centuries——"

"Ever since the alderman tipped King James for the title?" asked Skinner.

"Well, it's jolly valuable, from the fuss old Popper is

making about it," said Hobby. "Tankards and goblets and things—all sorts of stuff! The man, whoever he was, seems to have made a pretty good clearance. Old Popper thinks it was Leech——"

"He saw him?" asked Harry.

"Well, he saw him, but only for a tick, as he jumped from the window, from what I hear," said Hobby. "He can't swear that it was Leech, but he's convinced that it was, from what I hear."

"That won't do for a judge and jury!" remarked Vernon-Smith.

"Hardly!" grinned Bob.

"You know old Popper!" grinned Hobby. "He thinks he's the jolly old monarch of all he surveys. Look how he's grabbed that island in the Sark, and everybody jolly well knows it's public land, and always has been——"

"Never mind that island now—stick to the burglar!" said Stewart of the Shell. "What have they done to Leech?"

"Old Popper got Grimey on the phone, so they say," answered Hobby. "He told them it was Leech, and the peelers went straight to the man's lodgings in Bridge Street, at Courtfield. He was out, but they got him when he came in. But he had nothing on him. He was taken to the station, but they had to let him go again—there was nothing to go on."

"If he was out in the middle of the night it looks a bit suspicious," remarked Johnny Bull. "But they couldn't hold a man on that."

"What time was it, Hobby?"

"Between one and two in the morning."

"Not the time a chap generally goes for a walk!" said the Bounder. "Did Leech say where he had been?"

"Oh, yes. It's all over the place," said Hobby. "He had a toothache, and couldn't sleep, and went out to walk it off."

"Bit of a coincidence," said Smithy. "But they can't worry him much without something better than that."

"Any more evidence, Hobby?"

"Not that I've heard of," said Hobson. "They say that Leech has been at the Peal of Bells to-day—after the police let him go—telling everybody that old Popper's put this on him, because he answered him back when he was sacked."

"Old Popper wouldn't do anything of the kind," said Harry. "But he's just the old ass to believe anything against a man who was cheeky. He ought to have made sure before he accused the man."

"Catch old Popper stopping to make sure, once his giddy back was up!" grinned Hobby. "They're saying in Courtfield that he's fearfully shirty about the man being let go, though there's nothing to detain him on. Still, he's a decent old boy, in his way. He won't swear to a burglar's identity, as he can't be positive that it was Leech he saw jumping from the window. He's sure of it, but not enough to swear to it as a positive fact. He thinks that his jolly old lordly will and pleasure is enough to detain the man on—but the police don't seem to agree."

"And, all the while, the man who did it is getting quietly away?" remarked Skinner.

"I shouldn't wonder."

"Old Popper's an ass!" said Skinner. "If it was Leech, he couldn't have known the police would have been waiting at his lodgings for him. He would have walked in with the loot, and they'd have had it."

"Of course they would!" agreed Hobby.

"Cheeky old ass!" said Coker of the Fifth. Coker had joined the crowd listening to Hobby's thrilling news. "He's got nothing against the man. If I were Leech, I'd jolly well bring an action against him."

"Oh, my hat!" said Hobson. "Could he?"

"Well, you can't call a man a thief without evidence," said Coker. "Old Popper would call anybody anything, when his back was up! That's the sort of cheeky old fossil he is. If it turns out that somebody else did it, Leech could bring an action."

"What a lark!" chuckled Skinner. "Fancy old Popper —had up in court by a sacked manservant!"

"Poor old Popper!"

Harry Wharton & Co. left the group of fellows, discussing the latest excitement, and went to look for Billy Bunter. In the light of Hobby's news, it looked as if Bunter's tale might have, at least, some slight foundation of fact.

They found the fat Owl blinking at the tuckshop window. As it was more than an hour since dinner, Billy Bunter's fat thoughts were, naturally, turning on food. He blinked round hopefully at the chums of the Remove through his big spectacles.

"I say, you fellows, my postal order hasn't come!" said the fat Owl. "I believe I told you fellows I was expecting a postal order."

"I fancy I've heard something of it," said Harry Wharton, laughing. "But never mind your postal order now——"

"The fact is, I'm stony!" said Bunter. "Actually short of money. If you fellows could lend me five bob till my postal order comes——"

"Chuck it! Look here, you fat ass, we've just heard that there was a burglary at Popper Court last night," said Harry.

"I told you so!" answered Bunter. "The man dodged them by swimming off to the island——"

"Well, as he seems to have dodged them, I suppose it doesn't matter much whether he did it by swimming to the island or not," said Harry. "But if it's true, the police want to know. Did it really happen?"

"I've told you it did!" howled Bunter.

"Yes, but that looks as if it didn't!"

"Beast!"

"If it really happened, you'd better go and tell Quelch!" said the captain of the Remove. "I don't suppose it's of much consequence which way the man went, as he got away, but you never can tell. If you saw anything at all of the burglar, Quelch ought to be told, and he can decide whether to pass it on to old Grimey."

"Only tell him the truth!" urged Nugent. "Leave out the film bits."

"Chuck the revolvers, and knives, and machine-guns, and things!" suggested Bob Cherry. "Keep to the facts —if any!"

"Yah!"

"You fellows coming?" asked Coker, after class.

"Cricket?" asked Potter.

Potter of the Fifth knew perfectly well that Coker was not speaking of cricket. But he was desirous of keeping Coker off the subject of which his powerful mind was full.

"Don't be an ass!" said Coker gruffly. "You jolly well know——"

"I know the men are going down to the nets," said Greene. "Let's! You can do with a bit of practice, Coker."

But Coker was not to be deluded. At any other time, he might have fallen in the snare, but not this time. Coker was in a mood of deadly earnestness.

Coker had talked out of his hat that day! Like many fellows who talk out of their hats, he felt bound to make his words good.

He had said that he was going to Popper's Island after class. What he had said, he had said!

Dozens of fellows had heard him. If he did not make his words good, what were they going to think?

That Coker funked it!

That idea was intolerable! Even Coker, perhaps, realised that he had been a bit of an ass to blow off steam to such an extent. Still, in the heat of the moment, he had done it, and he was standing by it. That was as fixed and immutable as the laws of the Medes and Persians.

"Look here," said Coker, "don't beat about the bush! You know what I'm going to do. Old Popper——"

"Heard of the burglary at his place?" asked Greene.

It was a superfluous question, as everybody within ten miles of Popper Court had heard of the burglary by that time. Greene was simply trying to head Coker off the perilous topic.

"Never mind that!" said Coker. "I was going to say——"

"But it's a bit serious for old Popper!" remarked Potter. "They say a lot of giddy heirlooms were taken. The old bean is responsible for them! Silver goblets, dating from goodness knows when——"

"That island——"

"Oh, you've heard!" said Potter, deliberately leading Coker off the subject again. "That young ass, Bunter, of the Remove, was there all night——"

"I know that. I——"

"I mean, he makes out that the burglar swam to the island, getting away from old Popper! I hear that he's told his Form-master——"

"Blow his Form-master, and Bunter, too!" roared Coker. "If you'll let a fellow speak——"

"But if he's told Quelch, I dare say there's something in it," remarked Greene. "I believe Quelch has phoned to Grimes, for what it's worth. What do you think, Coker? We wanted to ask your opinion."

This time Coker fell into the snare. He knew that his opinion, on any subject, was very valuable. Nobody else did, but Coker did.

"I shouldn't wonder," said Coker. "If they were hot at his heels it was rather a cute dodge to swim off to the island and lie low till the coast was clear. Still, I wouldn't believe a word of that young ass Bunter. I dare say he dreamed it."

"He makes out that he heard the things clinking in the burglar's bag," said Potter. "Silver pots and things."

"Gammon, most likely," said Coker. "But I was going to say——" Coker headed back to the perilous subject.

"From what Bunter says, the man hid in that bunch of willows at the landing-place on the island quite near him!" said Potter. "He never saw Bunter, and——"

"Bet you the funky young ass took care he didn't!" sniffed Coker. "But never mind that. I——"

54

"I gather that he lay very low and waited for the man to clear," said Potter, keeping to the subject.

He was not particularly interested in that subject, but he would have talked on any subject from the League of Nations to the influence of blue in the arts to keep Coker off the subject Coker wanted to get at.

"Bet you he did!" grunted Coker. "If it's true! Most likely it isn't! But I was saying——"

"And he heard old Popper and his man Joyce on the bank, talking," said Greene. "The burglar must have heard them, too. If he was there, I mean, as Bunter says. I shouldn't wonder if Grimes makes something out of that."

"How do you mean?" asked Coker.

"Well, suppose it was Leech," said Greene.

"I don't suppose it was!" said Coker.

"But suppose it was, and it happened as that young ass Bunter is telling everybody who will listen, then that accounts for his not walking into his lodgings with the loot!" said Greene.

"I don't see that it does!" said Coker.

"Well, hearing old Popper gabbling, as Bunter says he did, he would know the peelers would be ready for him when he got home. He would jolly well park his loot in a safe place before he went back to his lodgings."

"Bet you old Grimes jumps on that!" said Potter. "I dare say he will want to see Bunter about it. Think so, Coker?"

But even Coker, by this time, realised that his friends were deliberately keeping up a discussion on an unimportant topic for no other purpose than to waste time—in other words, to keep Coker out of mischief.

"Look here," said Coker, "chuck it! Are you coming with me to Popper's Island or not?"

It was a direct question, and it had to be answered. Potter and Greene answered it unmistakably.

"Not!" they said simultaneously.

"All right!" said Coker scornfully.

And he turned away, heading for the gates.

Potter and Greene exchanged a worried look and rushed after him. Coker did not stop, and they walked on either side of him, expostulating.

"Look here, Coker, old man, don't do it!" implored Greene. "Prout's pretty wild with you already——"

"That's nothing new!" sneered Coker.

"I believe Quelch has been talking to him about a man in his Form helping a Remove kid break bounds——"

"Blow Quelch!"

"Well, that makes Prout very wild, and——"

"He can be as wild as he likes, and I don't care a brass button!" said Coker. "I'm fed-up with Prout! Didn't I say before a crowd of fellows that I was going on Popper's Island this afternoon?"

"Yes; but——"

"Think I'm the fellow to back out!" demanded Coker disdainfully. "The Head ought never to have given in to old Popper to the extent of putting the island out of bounds. If he had asked me I should have advised him to tell old Popper where he got off, I can tell you."

"Oh, crumbs!" gasped Potter and Greene, almost overcome by the bare idea of the majestic Head of Greyfriars asking Horace Coker for advice.

"Every fellow in the school and every man-jack in the country," said Coker, "has a right on that island! I've a right, and I'm going to exercise it!"

"Yes, but it means a row!" said Greene.

"Let it!" said Coker. "I've been in rows before! I never get justice from Prout, as you know. I don't expect him to be pleased to see me standing up for the rights of the school. He ought to be; but I don't expect it of him."

"Coker, old chap——"

"Help me out with the boat!" said Coker.

"Oh, dear!"

They helped Coker out with the boat. He stood in it, bobbing by the school raft, and gave them a last stern look.

"Are you coming?"

"No jolly fear!" said Greene. "Don't do it, Coker! You know how jolly wild Prout is already! If he hears of it he——"

"You can tell him if you like!" retorted Coker.

"Don't be an ass! Old Popper might spot you on the island——"

"I'll be glad if he does! I want him to see that there's one Greyfriars man who isn't afraid of his airs and graces."

"He will report you to the Head——"

"I know that!"

"It might be a whopping——"

"Don't be an ass, Potter!"

"I've heard some of the fags saying that the old bean was watching the island yesterday. They were going there, but he scared them off."

"He won't scare me off!" said Coker disdainfully.

"For goodness' sake, Coker—— I tell you Prout will be hopping mad——"

"Let him hop!" said Coker.

He pushed off.

Potter and Greene stood on the raft, staring after him in dismay.

"The utter ass!" said Potter, "Oh, the howling chump!] It will very likely be a flogging if he's spotted."

"Might be the sack," said Greene.

"Perhaps he won't get there, though," added Potter, as he watched Coker's wobbly and uncertain course up the river. "It will take him all his time, the way he rows."

"He won't get there if there's anything on the river he can run into," agreed Greene.

And Coker's chums had to leave it at that; it was all they had left to hope for.

"Hem!" murmured Coker.

He made that monosyllabic remark thoughtfully.

Coker was on Popper's Island.

Perhaps because there had been nothing on the river for him to run into Coker had arrived at his destination.

He punted his boat in to the landing-place, stepped ashore, and tied the painter.

Looking out from the island, Coker had a view of the shining river, the towpath backed by the sweeping woods, and the red chimneys of Popper Court in the far distance.

But, with all his bulldog determination and truculence, Coker was rather glad that he had no view of Sir Hilton Popper or any of his keepers.

Thinking did not come easily to Coker of the Fifth. But he was thinking a little now. The outcome of his reflections was that he would prefer not to be spotted on that island.

He was prepared to defy Sir Hilton Popper to the uttermost lengths. He was even prepared, if sufficiently provoked, to dot the baronet on his aristocratic nose. The mere sight of Sir Hilton, the mere sound of his authoritative bark, would have been sufficient to rouse the warlike blood of the Cokers in his veins.

But there were other considerations. He was breaking bounds. Thoughtless fellows who went out of bounds were given lines or detentions. But after the way Prout had talked of him that day Coker's action could not be regarded as a thoughtless and careless one, it would be regarded as a deliberate act of defiance—as, indeed, it was.

Coker had to keep his word. He was not going to have Greyfriars fellows saying that he had bragged of what he was going to do, and funked it when the pinch came. Not Coker.

Still, Coker rather hoped that he would not be spotted on the forbidden island, and reported at Greyfriars.

He was keeping his word. He was, rather, making his boast good. He had said, for all Greyfriars to hear, that he was going to that island after class, that he was going to sit there, and let old Popper come along and spot him if he liked! He was doing it!

If "old Popper" turned up, Coker was prepared to hurl defiance in his teeth! Nevertheless, he had rather a secret hope that old Popper wouldn't turn up! He hardly admitted it to himself, but there it was.

He sat on the island, leaning against the very tree on which Billy Bunter had propped his fat form the night before.

Splash!

Coker gave a little start at the sound of an oar on the river above the island.

A boat was coming down the Sark, from the direction of Courtfield Bridge. Coker set his jaw grimly.

If that boat passed on the side of the island where he was sitting, the boatman would see him. If the boat belonged to Popper Court, he would be reported as a trespasser.

Perhaps a temptation assailed the bull-headed Horace to slip out of sight for a few minutes in the willows.

If so, he resisted it.

He was not going to skulk out of sight! He was going to do what he said that he would do!

Coker sat tight.

Truculent and determined as Coker was, perhaps he was relieved to find that the boat did not pass. As it did not come into sight, he concluded that it had gone by on the other side of the island.

But a few minutes later there was a sound of rustling in the trees and thickets near at hand.

Coker stared round.

The boat, after all, had not passed. It had stopped at the island, though not on Coker's side of it.

Whoever was in it had landed, and was coming across the island.

That was rather odd, for anyone who wanted to get to that side of the island could easily have landed there, and saved himself the trouble of pushing his way through the thick underwoods to get across.

But it occurred to Coker that the newcomer, whoever he was, did not want to be spotted from the Popper Court side.

Coker did not care who it was, though he was, in his heart of hearts, glad that it was likely to be nobody from

Popper Court. Anyone from that establishment, of course, would not have cared whether he was seen or not—as this newcomer apparently did.

In a few minutes the newcomer emerged from the thickly wooded interior of the island, and Coker saw him.

He was a youngish man, with a smooth, clean-shaven face, dressed quietly in dark clothes. Coker would have taken him for some sort of manservant, on his looks.

The man did not see Coker, for the moment, sitting under the tree. He made straight for the clump of willows growing over the edge of the water.

As he reached them he gave a sharp, stealthy look round, with eyes as wary as a cat's, and that wary glance fell on the staring Coker.

The man gave a startled exclamation. It was clear that he had feared to be observed from the towpath; but had not expected to see anyone on the island itself.

Coker stared at him in blank wonder.

The man had landed on the island, pushed across through the thickets, and made direct for that clump of willows—for what imaginable reason Coker could not even begin to guess. There was nothing in the willows, so far as Coker could see, to interest anybody.

The man stepped towards him quickly.

"Who are you?" he exclaimed. "What are you doing here?"

"Sitting under this tree!" answered Coker coolly. "What the dickens does it matter to you?"

"You are trespassing here!"

"Rot!" answered Coker.

"There is a board up on this island—'Trespassers will be Prosecuted'!"

"That's only old Popper's cheek!" answered Coker. "I'm not taking any notice of that! You don't seem to be taking much notice of it yourself!"

"You had better go!" said the man. "Sir Hilton Popper is very particular about anyone landing on this island. I see you have a boat—you had better go at once!"

Coker simply stared at him.

"You clear me off this island!" roared Coker to the man from Courtfield

He would not have cleared off the island if Sir Hilton Popper, Baronet, had ordered him to do so in his own lordly person. So he was not likely to take such orders from this nobody.

"Do you hear me?" snapped the smooth-faced man. His manner was a strange mixture of angered uneasiness.

"I'm not deaf!" answered Coker.

"Well, are you going?"

"No fear!"

The man stood eyeing him. His glance shifted from Coker, and wandered across to the lonely towpath and the woods beyond. Then it returned to Coker. Coker rose to his feet, without, however, the slightest intention of getting into his boat. This fellow's cool cheek in fancying that he could order him off, annoyed Coker.

"You'd better go!" said the man, after a pause.

"I shall please myself about that!" retorted Coker. "Who the dickens are you?"

"Will you go?"

"No, I won't!"

The man breathed hard.

"I don't want to lay hands on you," he said. "But I don't want you here. If you don't go, I shall pitch you into your boat! Now are you going?"

Coker's eyes blazed.

"You try it on!" he roared. "By gum, I'd like to see you try it on!"

The next moment Coker had his wish! The man leaped at him, grasped him, and whirled him towards the boat. Coker, taken by surprise, staggered in his grasp.

But that was only for a moment. The next moment Horace Coker rallied, and gave grasp for grasp, and if the man from Courtfield fancied that he was a schoolboy to be easily handled, he found out his mistake very quickly. They struggled on the water's edge, staggering to and fro, till Coker's foot caught in a trailing willow root, and he rolled over. But he did not let go, and he dragged his adversary with him, and they rolled together, splashing, in the muddy shallows under the willows.

The Last Straw!

"I SAY, you fellows!" yelled Billy Bunter. "He's gone!"

"Who's gone, fathead, and where?" asked Bob Cherry.

"Coker!" gasped Bunter. "Gone to Popper's Island! He said he would, and he jolly well has!"

Billy Bunter did not see Prout!

Bunter seldom saw anything until it was right under his little fat nose. Mr. Prout, of course, was not under his nose! So the fat Owl of the Remove did not see him.

Prout was walking majestically in the quad after class, with a frown on his plump brow. He was, in point of fact, thinking about Coker. He had been annoyed with Coker all day. Coker had, as usual, given him trouble in the Form-room—added to his already great offence. Mr. Quelch had spoken to Prout, sharply and acidly, on the subject of Coker, which fanned the flame of Prout's wrath; Prout, like all beaks, hated to have another beak finding fault with his Form.

In those very moments when Billy Bunter yelled out his startling news, Prout was thinking that he had been very lenient with Coker, in letting him off with an impot —too lenient! So Bunter's excited squeal had the effect of making Prout start like a horse stung by a wasp. The portly Prout came to a halt in his stately pacing, spun round, and fixed his eyes on the fat Owl of the Remove.

"I say, you fellows, he's really gone!" squealed Bunter. "He was bragging that he would; and you know Coker—catch him owning up that he was gassing! He's gone up to Popper's Island!"

Prout stood like a portly statue.

If this was true, it was the last straw—the very last!

"Shut up, you blithering owl!" hissed Bob Cherry. "Prout's listening to every word you're saying!"

"Oh, crikey!" gasped Bunter.

He blinked round through his big spectacles.

Prout came towards him.

"Coker's at the nets, isn't he?" remarked Bob Cherry to his friends—for the benefit of Prout as he approached.

"I saw him with Potter and Greene," said Harry Wharton, catching on to the idea and playing up.

"Coker's pretty keen on getting Blundell to shove him into the Fifth Form eleven," remarked Johnny Bull. "Let's go and see what he's doing at the nets."

"Coker's always worth watching at cricket!" said Nugent.

"The worthfulness is terrific!" said Hurree Jamset Ram Singh. "Let us proceed to watch the esteemed Coker at his absurd cricket!"

It was a kind attempt to side-track Prout. But it booted not! Prout had heard every word squealed out by the fat Owl of the Remove, and he was not to be side-tracked.

Taking no notice of the Famous Five, he boomed at the fat junior.

"Bunter!"

"Oh, lor'!" said Bunter.

"I heard what you said, Bunter!"

"I—I didn't say anything, sir!" stammered Bunter.

"I heard you state that Coker of my Form has gone to Popper's Island. Are you aware of this as a fact?"

"Oh! No, sir!" gasped Bunter. "I—I didn't mean exactly that he had gone to Popper's Island, sir! I—I meant that—that he hadn't, sir!"

"You meant that he had not when you stated that he had!" gasped Prout.

"Yes, sir! That's it! I say, Toddy's calling me——"

"Stand where you are, Bunter! Answer me! Did you see Coker of my Form going to Popper's Island?"

"No, sir! I wasn't on the raft when he started, and I

never heard Potter and Greene trying to stop him! I—I think Coker's gone out on his bike, sir—that stink-bike of his, sir! I—I believe he's gone over to Lantham."

"Upon my word!" gasped Prout. "Bunter, I gather from your words that Coker of my Form declared his intention of going to that island."

"Oh, no, sir! He never said anything about it—not a word! These fellows can tell you the same, sir. They were here, and heard him——"

Mr. Prout gave Bunter a look, uttered a snort, and stalked away. Harry Wharton & Co. also gave Bunter looks—very expressive looks.

"You gabbling ass!" said Bob Cherry. "You've given that born idiot Coker away to his beak!"

"Oh, really, Cherry——"

"Has he really gone up to the island?" asked Harry.

Bunter grinned.

"Yes, rather! He's gone all right! But it's all right about Prout! I've stuffed Prout!"

"You've stuffed him!" gasped Nugent.

"You heard me tell him Coker had gone out on his stink-bike!" said Bunter. "Easy enough to stuff Prout!"

"You howling ass!" said Johnny Bull.

"Oh, really, Bull——"

"This will mean a fearful row for Coker!" said Bob. "Prout's wild with him already for putting Bunter on the island yesterday. Coker's the man to ask for trouble, and no mistake. Likely enough old Popper will spot him there. He was prowling about yesterday on the watch."

"Yesterday was a half-holiday," said Harry. "Besides, old Popper has something else to think about now after a burglary at his house. Coker's a blithering idiot, but that's no reason why Bunter should howl it out to his beak!"

"I never saw Prout!" said Bunter. "Besides, I've stuffed him all right——"

"Oh, bump him!"

"I saw, you fellows—— Yarooooooh!" roared Billy Bunter.

Bump!

"Yoooo-hoooop!"

"Give him another!"

"Yow-ow-woop!"

Again, and then again, Billy Bunter was bumped, and his yells could be heard far and wide.

Bumping Bunter was satisfactory in its way. But the harm was done now; there was no doubt about that. From a distance the Famous Five observed Prout rolling down to the cricket ground, where Potter and Greene were at practice with some of the Fifth. They guessed easily enough that he was going to ask them where Coker was.

Prout was seen to speak to Potter and Greene. Both of them looked very uncomfortable. Neither was likely to give Coker away if he could help it; but the utmost they could say was that they did not know where Coker was— which was true enough, for they were by no means sure that a fellow who rowed as Coker did would reach his destination in a boat.

Prout's next peregrination took him down to the boat-house. No doubt he learned there, from the boat-keeper, that Coker had taken his boat out, for his plump brow was like thunder as he came back to the House.

A little later the Famous Five, in the quad, glimpsed Prout—through the open window of the Head's study. Prout was in that study with Dr. Locke.

"Gentlemen, chaps, and sportsmen," said Bob Cherry, "I shouldn't like to be in Coker's shoes when he comes back from Popper's Island!"

And the Co. agreed that they wouldn't, either. It was plain that a storm awaited Horace Coker when he came back from his trip, and it was not going to be a mere summer gale, but a terrific thunderstorm!

"Ow!" howled Coker.

Splash!

Crash!

Coker, struggling valiantly in the grasp of the man who was seeking to clear him off Popper's Island, went down heavily, dragging the man after him.

They splashed together, Coker underneath.

There was shallow water under the willows on the edge of Popper's Island. There was more mud than water close up to the willows.

Right into that sea of mud went Coker, crashing and splashing, with the man from Courtfield sprawling over him.

Crashing into thick mud was not nice. But it was not the mud that caused Coker to utter that howl of anguish.

His head banged on something hard in the mud.

Mud, as a rule, though nasty to fall into, was soft. Under the willows it was very soft—wet and clammy and oozy. Coker might reasonably have expected to fall soft in such a spot—instead of which, his bullet head banged on something very hard under the mud, and it hurt.

What it was his head had banged on Coker did not know. It was the back of his head that banged, and he had, of course, no eyes in the back of his head. But though he did not know what the hard object was, he knew that it hurt, and he roared.

And he heaved. Already angry at this fellow's cheek in thinking that he could turn him off the island, Coker was by now fearfully enraged—between splashing in mud and banging his head. He heaved fiercely and furiously, splashing mud and water right and left.

The assailant was pitched off. Panting, the man from Courtfield scrambled out of the mud, and Coker scrambled after him.

Coker was breathless, but he did not pause for breath. He hurled himself on the smooth-faced man.

Hammer-and-tongs, they went at it.

Coker was a hefty fellow. He was remarkably hefty. He had a punch like a steam-hammer. He had unlimited pluck and unlimited beef. He could have given a good account of himself in a tussle with a bargee. And the smooth-faced man was no athlete. Neither did he seem to be over-endowed with pluck or a capacity to take punishment. He was a man against a boy, but he very

67

soon realised that he had taken too much for granted—much too much.

Coker knocked him right and left.

Coker captured some punishment, for the man from Courtfield hit hard and hit often. But he handed out more than he received. The smooth face was hardly recognisable after a few of Coker's terrific punches had landed thereon.

Who the man was, and what he was after, Coker neither knew nor cared. All he knew was that the cheeky rat had tried to pitch him off the island, smothered him with mud, and banged his head. That was enough for Coker! He was jolly well going to show this cheeky rotter who was who, and what was what!

And he jolly well did!

Twice the man from Courtfield went down, and jumped up again, and renewed the strife. His nose was streaming crimson, and crimson ran from a corner of his mouth, and one of his eyes was closed and blackening. A third time he went down, and when he scrambled up, he backed off. It looked as if he had had enough.

Coker hadn't! He followed his enemy up, still punching.

Back and back went the infuriated man, followed by the equally infuriated Coker, hitting out like a hammer.

He fairly took to his heels at last, and scuttled away through the underwood, across the island, like a rabbit.

After him charged Coker.

"Stop!" roared Coker. "You rotten funk! You sneaking worm! Stop! I'll smash you! I'll spiflicate you! Stop!"

The panting man did not stop. He fled wildly. He crashed through thickets, and reached the other side of the little island.

A boat was tied up there to a branch; the boat in which the man had come down the river. He leaped into it, with Coker only a yard behind him.

He tore the painter loose, and the boat rocked out on the river. Coker made a grab at it and missed, and barely escaped tumbling over into the Sark.

The man from Courtfield grabbed the oars and rowed. He glared back at Coker as he went, pulling across the river to the distant bank. Coker brandished a fist after him.

"Come back!" he bawled. "You'll turn me off this island, will you, you cheeky snipe? Come back and do it!"

But it was clear that the man from Courtfield had had enough of turning the hefty Horace off the island. He pulled hard, and the boat shot away across the Sark, and disappeared under the fringe of trees on the opposite bank.

Coker panted.

He would have been glad if the snipe had come back! He wanted to give him some more. But the man was not coming back—not so long as Coker was there, at all events.

"Cheeky cad!" gasped Coker. "Trespassing himself, by gum, if it's trespassing here—and trying to turn me off! I wish I'd given him a few more."

Coker turned and tramped back across the island.

He reached the landing-place on the Popper Court side, gasping for breath, streaming with perspiration, and reeking with mud. He stopped by the water's edge to bathe his burning face.

"Cheeky cad!" gasped Coker, as he rose from bathing his heated face, and rubbed it with his handkerchief.

Then he rubbed the back of his head.

There was a bruise there, from the bang he had had when he pitched into the mud under the willows. It was rather painful.

"Great pip!" gasped Coker suddenly.

From the shallows under the drooping willows an object showed up—the hard object on which Coker had banged his head!

Coker stared at it blankly.

He had rather wondered what his head had banged on, in soft mud. Now he saw what it was. It was an attache-case!

That attache-case, evidently, had been sunk in the shallow mud under the willows.

It had lain there unseen, hidden by mud.

Coker had crashed in the mud and banged his head on it. That, and the scramble afterwards, had dislodged it. One end was sticking up.

In sheer amazement, Coker stared at it. It was the very last thing he would have expected to see there.

Coker was not quick on the uptake. But even Coker's brain worked. It dawned on him slowly, but it did dawn on him, that that attache-case was what the man from Courtfield had been after. He had come across the island direct for the willows, for no reason that Coker could guess at the time. But the reason was plain now. It was, in fact, sticking out of the mud under Coker's eyes!

Had not Coker been there, the smooth-faced man would have disinterred that attache-case from the mud, and taken it away in his boat. And he had tried to clear Coker off, because he did not want anyone to see him doing it! Slowly but surely this dawned on Coker.

"By gum!" said Coker.

Some time or other that smooth-faced man had hidden that attache-case in the mud under the willows. Now he had come back for it. When—and why? Back into Coker's mind came Bunter's tale—of the fugitive who had crouched in those willows the night before, with a bag of plunder from Popper Court.

"Oh, crikey!" said Coker.

He trod into the mud, grabbed the attache-case, and dragged it out. It was very heavy. A clinking sound came from inside it as Coker dumped it down on the grass.

Another moment, and it was open.

"Great pip!" gurgled Coker.

He blinked dizzily at shining silver! Tankards, goblets, all sorts of silverware were packed in that attache-case.

"The—the—the burglar!" stuttered Coker. "I—I've been scrapping with the burglar! Oh, crikey!"

In dizzy astonishment Horace Coker blinked at the historic silver plate of Popper Court.

"Oh, crikey!" he repeated.

He closed the attache-case, secured it, and lifted it into his boat. Then he pushed off from Popper's Island. Coker had made good his boast—he had landed on the island, and sat there in defiance of all the Poppers in the universe. He had intended to stay longer. But what he chiefly needed now was a wash and a change—also, the loot had to be handed over into safe keeping. So Coker pulled away down the river to the Greyfriars boathouse—happily unaware of what awaited him there!

"Hallo, hallo, hallo!"

"Here he comes!"

"Here comes Coker!"

"I say, you fellows, Prout's got his eye on him——"

"Poor old Coker!"

Fifty pairs of eyes, at least, were fixed on Horace Coker, as he pulled down to the Greyfriars raft, catching crabs not a few as he pulled.

Among them gleamed the baleful eyes of Mr. Prout.

Prout stood portly, pompous, dignified—and wrathy. It was a very serious matter from Prout's point of view. From the point of view of others, it was less serious, and some of the fellows were grinning.

Half Greyfriars, if not all, knew of Coker's reckless boast that day. So when the news spread that Coker was playing up to it, and that his beak was on his track, the general interest centred in Horace.

Prout was there to grab him when he came. Everybody else was there to see Prout grab him. Opinions differed as to what was going to happen to Coker. From Prout's expression, it might have been something lingering, with boiling oil in it. Lines or detentions, obviously, would be too mild. Was it going to be a flogging—a flogging in the Fifth? Or even the sack?

Interest was very keen, and the excitement grew as Coker was sighted. Having his back to his audience as he pulled, Coker did not discover them till he was very near.

But as the boat ranged up to the raft, Coker became

71

aware that he was the cynosure of uncounted eyes.

He stared in surprise.

Potter pulled in the boat for him. Greene tied the painter. Coker stepped out, lifting after him a rather heavy attache-case.

Fellows stared at that attache-case. They had not expected Coker to come back with luggage.

"I say, you fellows, he's been on a picnic!" squeaked Billy Bunter.

"Well, he's got a nerve!" said Bob Cherry.

The attache-case looked as if Coker had carried supplies of some sort. No one, naturally, guessed that he had disinterred that attache-case from the mud under the willows on Popper's Island.

"Coker!" Prout boomed.

Then Horace became aware of the portly figure overtopping the crowd. So far, Coker had not guessed that his exploit was known at the school. He guessed it now.

"Oh!" gasped Coker. "Yes, sir!"

"You have returned!" boomed Prout.

That question hardly needed an answer. Coker was big enough to be seen! But Coker answered:

"Yes, sir!"

"I do not desire," boomed Prout, "to condemn you unheard, Coker! If you have merely been on the river, Coker, rowing in your boat. I have nothing to say to you, Coker. But I have reason to suspect that you have deliberately and intentionally added to the offence you have already given by trespassing on the property of Sir Hilton Popper. I require to know, Coker, and at once, whether you have done this."

Coker's jaw set square.

"No, sir!" he answered.

Prout looked at him. There was a general gasp. Everybody knew that Coker had been to Popper's Island—Potter and Greene best of all. So Coker's reply caused general amusement. Coker had his faults, but he was the last fellow in the world to lie himself out of a scrape. Coker would have snorted with scorn at the idea.

"You—you have not, Coker?" exclaimed Prout.

"Certainly not, sir! I should refuse to put a foot on Sir Hilton Popper's property if he asked me!" answered Coker firmly.

Then Coker's meaning dawned on the eager listeners-in. It was not always easy to get at Coker's meaning, even when he did mean anything. But they got on to it now. Coker did not regard the island in the Sark as Sir Hilton Popper's property, and wasn't going to pretend that he did.

"Coker!" boomed Prout. "I have good reason—good reason to believe that you have been on Popper's Island. But if you assure me that you have not done so, I am bound to take the word of a boy in my Form."

Fellows waited breathlessly for Coker's answer.

"I didn't say that, sir!" said Coker calmly. "I said I hadn't been on Sir Hilton Popper's property, and I haven't! I've been on the island in the Sark."

"Good old Coker!" murmured Bob Cherry.

"Good old fathead!" said Johnny Bull.

"That island, sir, is public land, as I mentioned when you were speaking about it this morning!" said Coker.

"Jevver hear a man ask for it like this?" murmured the Bounder.

"Never!" sighed Bob.

Prout breathed hard. He breathed deep. His portly face assumed a purple hue. If he had been wrathy before, he was towering now.

"Coker!" he gasped. "Do not bandy words with me, Coker! Do not bandy words with your Form-master, Coker! Have you, or have you not, trespassed on the property of Sir Hilton Popper?"

"No, sir!" said Coker firmly.

Coker was the man to stick to his guns.

Prout almost choked.

"Have you, or have you not, landed on the island in the river, called Popper's Island?" he gurgled.

Coker had fairly forced him to put it Coker's way!

"Yes, sir!" answered Coker.

"Enough!" boomed Prout. "After my words to you this morning, after the punishment inflicted upon you, you have ventured to do this. You have trespassed on Sir Hilton's property, and——"

"No sir! I——"

"Silence!" roared Prout. "I will not allow you to argue with me, Coker! I will not permit you to bandy words! You have landed on the island belonging to Sir Hilton Popper——"

"It doesn't belong to him, sir! You see——"

"Silence! Not only have you landed there, but you have, I conclude, picnicked there!" Prout glanced at the attache-case, and drew from it the same conclusion as the other observers. "No doubt you have strewn the island with empty bottles and such things, in the manner often complained of by the owner——"

"Oh, no, sir! Sir Hilton Popper isn't the owner——"

"Shut up, for the love of Mike!" hissed Potter, in Coker's ear.

"Don't be an ass, Potter! I have to answer my Form-master when he speaks to me," said Coker. "What do you mean?"

"Follow me!" boomed Prout. "Follow me, Coker! I shall take you to your headmaster! I have already consulted Dr. Locke on the subject of this flagrant defiance of authority and the laws of property. Your headmaster will deal with you. I wash my hands of you!"

"I'd better tell you, sir——"

Coker picked up the attache-case.

"Follow me!"

"But this, sir——"

"I have ordered you to follow me, Coker, to your headmaster. Will you do so, or will you not?" boomed Prout.

"Oh, certainly, sir, but if you'd look into this——"

"Follow me this instant!" roared Prout.

He turned and stalked away. Coker stared after him, and then followed, the attache-case in his hand.

After Coker marched an army of Greyfriars fellows, greatly excited.

"It's the sack this time!" Potter murmured to Greene. "Prout's just boiling over."

Greene nodded gloomily.

All Right for Coker!

DR. LOCKE fixed his eyes on Coker of the Fifth, as his Form-master marched him into the study.

His eyes dwelt on Coker with grim disapproval. He noted his muddy clothes and boots, his swollen nose, and his darkened eye. He glanced at the muddy attache-case in his hand.

Coker's *tout ensemble* was not pleasing to the view. His best friend would not have said that he looked, at that moment, a credit to any school. In point of fact, he looked absolutely disreputable.

"Here, sir," boomed Prout, "is Coker! You see, sir, the state in which he has returned! A disgraceful state! He has admitted, sir, that he has transgressed school bounds—that he has trespassed on the property of Sir Hilton Popper——"

"Oh, no, sir!" said Coker. "I've only been on the island in the river, sir."

Prout gurgled.

"You hear him, sir! You hear his argumentative impertinence——"

"You may leave this headstrong and rebellious boy to me, Mr. Prout," said the Head, in icy tones. "Coker!"

"Yes, sir!"

75

"You have landed on the island in the river?"

"Yes, sir! As public land——"

"Silence! You have, from your disgraceful appearance, been fighting?"

"I had a bit of a scrap, sir. A man had the cheek to try to turn me off the island——"

"Upon my word!" exclaimed the Head. "You have not only trespassed on the island, but you have forcibly resisted Sir Hilton's keepers——"

"He wasn't a keeper, sir!"

"With whom, then, have you been fighting?" demanded the Head sternly.

Perhaps he had an awful misgiving that Coker's victim might have been the lofty lord of Popper Court himself! Really, he would hardly have been surprised had Coker answered "Sir Hilton Popper."

But Coker's answer, when it came, made him jump.

"A burglar, sir!"

"What does this boy mean, Mr. Prout?" asked the Head blankly.

"Do not ask me, sir. I cannot tell you, sir! This boy's stupidity—his astounding obtuseness—it is beyond me, sir!"

"Coker!" gasped the Head. "What do you mean?"

"Only what I say, sir!" answered Coker, in mild surprise. "I didn't know he was the burglar when he tackled me, but I guessed afterwards——"

"What burglar?" almost shrieked the Head.

"The one who burgled Popper Court last night, sir!" explained Coker.

Dr. Locke gazed at him speechless. Mr. Prout made inarticulate noises. Coker glanced from one to the other.

"You see, sir," he explained, "I thought the fellow was just some cheeky rat at first, trying to turn me off the island, and I jolly well whopped him! He was glad to clear off, sir. I'd have copped him, if I'd known he was the burglar at the time; but he was gone——"

Dr. Locke recovered his breath.

"A—a—a man desired to turn you off the island, and

"Can you state, Coker, that the stolen silver is hidden on Popper's Island?" asked the Head

you—you fancy that he—he was a burglar?" he stuttered.

"I jolly well knew he was, sir, when I found out that he had come back to the island for the loot!" said Coker.

"The—the loot!" said the Head dazedly.

"Yes, sir. He must have parked it there last night when Bunter was there, and——"

"Is this boy sane, Mr. Prout?" asked the Head.

"I hardly know, sir," gasped Prout—"I hardly know!"

"Coker, have you any reason—have you the slightest or remotest reason—to suppose that the articles stolen from Popper Court last night were hidden on the island in the Sark?"

"Yes, sir—rather!" said Coker. "I jolly well banged my head on the bag—I know that. You see, sir, it's pretty clear now that the fellow was on the island just as Bunter said, and, knowing that he would be watched for, he hid the stuff there, and came back for it this afternoon when the coast was clear. If I'd known it at the time, I'd have snaffled him, too. But I never knew till after he was gone."

"Coker, can you state, as a fact, that the stolen silver from Popper Court is hidden on Popper's Island?" gasped the Head, while Mr. Prout stared dumbly at that hopeful member of his Form.

"Not now, sir," explained Coker. "It was there, sir, but it's here now."

"Here!" stuttered Dr. Locke.

"Yes, sir. I thought I'd better bring it away, in case that worm dodged back after it when I was gone."

"Bless my soul! Then where—what—how——"

"Here, sir!"

Coker opened the attache-case.

Dr. Locke gave a convulsive start. Mr. Prout almost bounded from the floor. Both of them fixed bulging eyes on the historic silver of Popper Court.

There was deep silence in the Head's study. A pin might have been heard to drop, for a long moment.

"Bless my soul!" said the Head feebly, at last.

Mr. Prout mumbled indistinctly.

"That's the lot, I think, sir," said Coker cheerfully. "It's just as the burglar parked it, anyhow. And luckily I was there and knocked him out before he could get his paws on it again. I thought I'd better bring it here, sir, for you to take care of till it can be sent back to Popper Court."

Dr. Locke looked at him. Then he looked at Prout.

Prout gasped.

"Sir, when I spoke to you on this subject, I—I certainly had the impression that this boy had gone to the island in defiance of authority. I had no idea—not the slightest idea—of this——"

"No doubt," assented the Head.

"The boy should have told me, sir—certainly he should have told me. Nevertheless, I think that even Sir Hilton Popper, sir, will be glad to hear of this boy—this boy of my Form, sir—visiting his island, for the purpose of recovering the stolen property."

"I should imagine so," said the Head.

Coker blinked.

"But I never knew——" he began.

The Head gave him a look.

"You need say no more, Coker," he said. "You may leave my study."

"Oh, certainly, sir; but I was only going to explain——"

"Leave my study, Coker!"

"Oh, yes, sir!"

Coker left it.

"What about fool's luck?" grinned Bob Cherry.

"Ha, ha, ha!"

The whole school chortled over it.

It was not the "sack" for Coker; it was not a whopping; it was not even lines or detentions. It was kudos. It was the spotlight.

Prout had an idea—perhaps he liked to have the idea —that a boy in his Form had spotted the missing loot which the police, so far, had failed to trace. Certainly Coker of the Fifth had recovered it. On that point there was no shadow of doubt. Prout was satisfied that a boy in his Form had brought credit upon himself, his Form, his Form-master, and his school. That was enough for Prout, which, in the circumstances, was fortunate for Horace Coker.

Even Sir Hilton Popper was satisfied when the missing silver was returned, safe and sound, to Popper Court. Inspector Grimes, calling at Greyfriars to question Billy Bunter on the subject of what the fat junior had seen during his night out, was astonished to be handed the bag of loot—the most astonished inspector in the whole police force.

But he was very satisfied, as well as astonished. Everybody, in fact, was satisfied, except the man Leech.

Leech, revisiting Popper's Island after dark that night, did not find his loot there. He found two men in blue waiting for him. And he found them even more troublesome than Coker, and did not succeed in getting away from them as he had got away from Coker.

So Leech, naturally, perhaps, did not share in the general satisfaction.

Coker was most satisfied of all. What he had said, he had said. What he had said he would do, he had done, and that was that. As for what would have happened to him but for that happy accident, Coker did not think of that. Thinking was not in Coker's line, which was, perhaps, just as well for him.

A Batting for Bolsover!

BILLY BUNTER hurled open the door of Coker's study in the Fifth Form passage at Greyfriars, and rushed in.

Bunter was in haste.

His fat face was crimson, and he puffed and he blew. He had come up the passage at top speed, and he hurtled into Coker's study like a fat cannon-ball.

Bunter bumped on the table, and clutched it for support, and gasped for breath.

"I—I say, Coker——" he spluttered.

Horace Coker of the Fifth Form uttered a sound that was like unto the trumpeting of a wild elephant in the jungle. Coker was seated at that table, working at a Latin exercise. The table rocked; the inkpot rocked; and a splash of ink went over Coker's exercise. Some of it went over Coker! Coker fairly roared with wrath.

"Why, you—you—you——"

Coker jumped up.

But for the table between, his grasp would have fallen at once on Bunter. Coker started round the table.

So did Billy Bunter, in the other direction.

The fat Owl of the Remove was breathless. But he was not too breathless to dodge Coker. Coker looked positively dangerous.

"I—I say, Coker, I—I came to tell you——" gasped Bunter, as he circled Coker's table.

"I'll smash you!" roared Coker, as he circled the table after Bunter.

"Bolsover's coming——"

"Look at my exercise!" roared Coker. "I'll teach you to rush into my study like a mad bull, and——"

81

D

"He's going to whop you——"

"What?"

"With a fives bat——"

"Eh?"

"I came to tell you!" gasped Bunter, still with the table between him and Coker. "He will be here in a minute! He says he's going to whop you, in your own study, with a fives bat."

Coker of the Fifth stopped in sheer astonishment.

"Whop me!" he gasped.

"Yes, old chap!" gasped Bunter. "I—I came to tip you——"

"A Remove fag—whop me!" stuttered Coker.

"He's coming."

There was a sound of tramping feet coming up the passage. Horace Coker stared blankly at Bunter, and then swung round towards the doorway. Somebody was coming up the passage—in haste! But Coker could hardly believe that it was Bolsover major of the Remove coming to whop a Fifth Form man in his study.

Bolsover was a big and hefty fellow—the biggest fellow in the Lower School. He was, in fact, bigger than a good many of the seniors. He was rather a bully, and had a heavy hand with small fags. He was cheeky to the Fifth; and Coker had more than once regarded him with a disapproving eye and thought that a thrashing would do him good.

But certainly it had never occurred to Horace Coker that Bolsover thought that a thrashing would do him good, and fancied that he could administer the same.

If Bolsover fancied that, Coker was the man to cure him.

"Mean to say——" gasped Coker.

"He's been bragging in the Remove passage that he's going to do it," panted the fat Owl. "You'll see him in a minute. He's got a fives bat——"

"I'll be glad to see him!" said Coker grimly.

He glared at the open doorway.

If Bolsover major of the Remove appeared there with

a fives bat in his hand Coker knew what he was going to do.

Tramp, tramp, tramp, came the heavy footsteps up the passage.

A figure appeared in the doorway.

It was that of Bolsover major, the bully of the Remove —with a red, excited face and a fives bat in his grasp. He glared into the study.

"Oh, there you are!" he roared as his eyes fell on Billy Bunter. And he rushed in.

The next moment Coker had him.

Up to that moment Coker had doubted. He could really hardly believe that any junior, even a big, head-strong, overbearing fellow like Bolsover major, could actually think of whopping him in his study. He was well aware that plenty of juniors would have liked to whop him. Coker prided himself on having a short way with fags; which did not, of course, make him popular among the fags. But that any junior could really think of whop-ping him was almost unimaginable to the great Coker.

But he could not doubt now—as the red and wrathy Removite rushed into his study, fives bat in hand.

He grasped Bolsover.

Big and hefty as Bolsover major was he was not so big and hefty as Coker of the Fifth. Coker whirled him off his feet and strewed him on the study carpet.

"Ow!" roared Bolsover as he went down. "Ow! Leggo! I——"

Coker's left hand grasped Bolsover's collar. Bolsover major's features grubbed into the carpet. Coker's right wrenched the fives bat from his hand.

Up went Coker's arm! Down it came! The fives bat banged on the Removite's trousers with a crack like a pistol-shot.

"Oooh!" roared Bolsover. "Urrggh!" He spluttered wildly, with his nose grinding into Coker's carpet. "Wurrgh! Leggo, you mad idiot! I—urrggh——"

Whack, whack!

"Gurrrggh!" gurgled the struggling junior. "Urrgh! I didn't—I wasn't—leggo—urrggh——"

"Oh, crikey!" gasped Bunter.

The fat junior gave the scene one blink through his big spectacles as he scuttled round the table. But he stayed only for one blink. Then he scuttled out of the study and his fleeing footsteps died away down the passage.

Coker did not heed him. And Bolsover major had no leisure to heed him, with his face grinding into a dusty carpet under Coker's grip, and the fives bat beating on his trousers.

"Whop me, eh?" roared Coker. "By Jove! Get on with it! I'd like to see any Remove fag whop me! I'd just like it! You've come to this study to whop me, have you? Who's getting the whopping? What?"

Whack, whack!

"Urrgh! Leggo! No! I haven't come——"

"Changed your mind!" grinned Coker. "I rather fancied you would, when you started on the job."

Whack, whack, whack!

"Yaroooh! I tell you, I was after Bunter!" yelled the wriggling Removite. "I saw him dodge into the Fifth, and came after him——"

Whack!

"Yarooop! I tell you, I caught him snaffling my toffee, and got after him with a fives bat!" shrieked Bolsover. "I tell you——"

Whack, whack, whack!

"Whooop! Yarooooh! Oh, crikey!"

It was useless for Bolsover to attempt to explain. Coker was not to be taken in.

Coker had, as a matter of fact, been taken in by the astute Owl of the Remove. But when an idea was once lodged in Coker's head, it was a fixture there. There was room in Horace Coker's powerful intellect for only one idea at a time. Having been convinced that Bolsover had come there with the cheeky intention of whopping him in his study, Coker was not open to conviction otherwise. He whacked and whacked.

Bolsover major struggled and wriggled and roared. Three or four Fifth Form men came up the passage, attracted by the uproar.

"Killing a pig in here, Coker?" asked Potter.

"What on earth's that game?" asked Greene.

"You'll have the roof down soon!" remarked Hilton.

Coker glanced round.

"This cheeky fag came here to whop me with a fives bat!" he said. "He looks like doing it, doesn't he?"

"Yow-ow! I never—— Yaroooooh!"

Whack, whack!

"I never—— Yurrrrrooop!"

"Looks like it—what?" grinned Coker. "What do you men think—eh?"

"Ha, ha, ha!"

Whack!

"You'd better not quite slaughter him, though!" remarked Potter. "Quelch would make a row if you polished off one of his young sweeps!"

Coker chuckled.

"Well, I think that will do!" he remarked. "You can have your bat, Bolsover." He shoved the fives bat down the back of the wriggling junior's neck. "Now you can cut! You men kick him down the passage!"

He heaved Bolsover major to the door. The bully of the Remove staggered into the passage. Potter and Greene and Hilton, grinning, kicked him as he passed, and Bolsover major tottered away.

"Come back again when you want to give me another whopping!" roared Coker derisively.

But Bolsover major was not thinking of whopping Coker. He was not thinking even of whopping Billy Bunter, much as that fat youth deserved it. He could hardly have whopped a fag of the Second Form just then. He tottered away, and Coker of the Fifth, in high good humour, strolled along to the games study, to tell the Fifth Form fellows there how a cheeky fag had come to his study to whop him, and what had happened to that cheeky fag.

"I say, you fellows! "

Billy Bunter squeaked his loudest, and Harry Wharton & Co., who were going out of gates, glanced round.

The fat Owl of the Remove was scuttling after them from the House, his little fat legs going like clockwork, his spectacles flashing back the rays of the June sun.

"Hold on! " squeaked Bunter.

The Famous Five obligingly held on. They were in no hurry, as they were only going for a ramble after class. If Billy Bunter wanted to join up for the ramble, they had no great objection, though they did not exactly pine for his fat company. They waited in the gateway for him to come up—which Bunter did, panting for breath.

"Going out?" he asked breathlessly.

"Oh, no! " said Johnny Bull sarcastically. "We've walked down to the gates because we're not going out! "

"Oh, really, Bull! I say, you fellows, if you're going to the pictures, I'll come! " gasped Bunter.

"But we're not! " said Frank Nugent.

"Bunshop?" asked Bunter hopefully.

"Not even the bunshop! " grinned Bob Cherry.

"Where, then?" demanded Bunter.

"Just a walk through Popper Court woods to the river, and back by the boathouse," answered Harry Wharton.

"What on earth for?"

The Famous Five chuckled.

There were quite good reasons for taking that walk. It was glorious June weather; there was sunshine, a blue sky, and a balmy breeze from the sea; the woods were shady and green and inviting, and walking was a good exercise.

But these good reasons were quite lost on Billy Bunter. Billy Bunter preferred to take his exercise sitting still. He never moved if he could help it—except his chin! Bunter's chin, it was true, seemed to have discovered the secret of perpetual motion. Why fellows should walk miles in order to get back to where they had started from had always been a mystery to Bunter.

"Look here," he said, "don't be asses! Stop in! "

"Fathead!" said Bob Cherry politely. "We're going out! Coming?"

"I say, hold on!" exclaimed Bunter. "I—I say, come up to the studies, and—and I'll do some of my ventriloquial tricks to—to amuse you—what?"

"Anybody want to stick in a study in this glorious weather to hear Bunter making weird noises with his neck?" asked Bob Cherry.

"Ha, ha, ha!"

The Famous Five walked out. Rather to their surprise, Billy Bunter rolled after them.

It was clear that Bunter did not want to go for a walk. But it seemed that he was keen on the company of the Famous Five—so keen that he was willing to exert himself for the sake of the same—which was very flattering, at all events.

"I say, you fellows, don't race!" exclaimed Bunter irritably.

The chums of the Remove were sauntering at their ease, but Bunter was a slow walker. He could have beaten a snail, but perhaps only an old, tired snail.

"Oh, dear!" grunted Johnny Bull. "Walk, if you're going to walk, fatty! Do you want us to crawl on our hands and knees?"

"Beast!"

Bunter puffed and blew. Several times he blinked back over a fat shoulder through his big spectacles. But he seemed more easy in his mind when the school gates were out of sight behind.

"What about sitting on this fence, you chaps?" he asked. "We could get a rest here till calling-over."

"Sit on it by all means!" said Bob Cherry. "We'll collect you when we come back!"

"Well, I don't want to lose your company!" said Bunter, rolling reluctantly on. "I always enjoy a walk with you fellows. You're such nice company!"

The Famous Five of the Remove looked at Bunter. They were willing to agree that they were nice company. They would have admitted that there was none better in the Greyfriars Remove. Still, they had not expected to hear it from Billy Bunter.

"What's the soft sawder for?" asked Johnny Bull.

"Oh, really, Bull——"

"Buck up, if you don't want to lose our nice company, Bunter!" said Harry Wharton, laughing. "We want to do more than two yards an hour!"

Billy Bunter bucked up. Once more he blinked back over a fat shoulder.

"Expecting somebody after you?" asked Frank Nugent.

"Oh, no! I'm not dodging that beast Bolsover!" said Bunter. "I came out with you fellows because I'm keen on a walk and I like your company."

"Ha, ha, ha!"

The mystery was solved now.

"Blessed if I see anything to cackle at!" grunted Bunter. "I fancy Bolsover won't be so full of beans when Coker's done with him. Still, I don't want a row with the brute. If he cuts up rusty when we get in, I shall expect my pals to stand by me."

"Why not cut off and warn them that they may be wanted?" asked Bob.

"Oh, really, Cherry——" Apparently, the Famous Five were the pals to whom Bunter alluded. "I say, as captain of the Remove, Wharton, you're bound to put down bullying! Quelch would expect it."

"Quelch won't be disappointed," said Harry cheerfully. "Who's been bullying whom?"

"That brute Bolsover!" said Bunter. "He got after me with a fives bat just before I came out. If I hadn't cut into Coker's study, he would have had me. Luckily, Coker fancied, for—for some reason, that Bolsover had come there to row with him and pitched into him. I left them scrapping."

"More power to both their giddy elbows!" said Bob heartily. "Both of them can do with a hiding!"

"Well, Bolsover may be very waxy about it," said Bunter. "I'd rather keep with you fellows for a bit. You can handle him all right."

"What have you been up to, you fat spoofer?" demanded Wharton.

"Nothing. The beast made out that I snaffled toffee in his study—and I wasn't in his study at all. I haven't been near his study. Besides, I only went there to speak to that French chap, Dupont."

"Oh, my hat!"

"But you know that cad Bolsover, he won't take a fellow's word! He's untruthful himself, that's the reason," said Bunter.

"Ha, ha, ha!"

"I say, you fellows, let's stop here!" The walkers had reached a spot in the lane where a stile gave access to a footpath through Popper Court woods. Billy Bunter blinked longingly at a sloping, grassy bank. "Let's sit down."

"The sit-downfulness is not the proper caper, my esteemed lazy Bunter!" grinned Hurree Jamset Ram Singh.

"Oh, really! I say, I'm not tired—I could walk you fellows off your legs, and chance it," declared Bunter. "But you know old Popper kicks up a fuss about people walking through his woods. Just as he does about people camping on his island and in the river. What's the good of hunting trouble?"

"Bow-wow!"

The Famous Five jumped over the stile, one after another. Billy Bunter cast another anxious blink backward before he followed.

There was no sign of pursuit. But Bunter decided not to risk it. He heaved his considerable weight over the stile.

The juniors followed the footpath towards the river, under the shady branches of old oaks and beeches. There were birds innumerable in the wood, and Sir Hilton Popper, of Popper Court, was very particular about his birds. That was not because he was fond of birds, his ultimate object being to find entertainment in shooting them! But until the time came for Sir Hilton to slaughter them with his own lofty hand he was very particular indeed about them, and anyone who disturbed Sir Hilton's birds was sure of Sir Hilton's terrific wrath.

"Oh, crikey!" ejaculated Bunter suddenly. "That's the old blighter!"

A hat showed over a thicket at a little distance. It was worn by some man coming through the wood, to emerge on the footpath.

Bunter halted in dismay.

"I say, you fellows!" he gasped. "That's old Popper, ten to one! He'll report us to the Head——"

"This is a public footpath, fathead," said Harry. "Even the Great Panjandrum can't turn anybody off it."

"You know that crusty old codger! He's always complaining about somebody or something, and the Head——"

"Might dodge the old ass!" murmured Bob.

Harry Wharton shook his head.

"We've a right here," he said.

"You silly asses!" squeaked Bunter. "If you want to get into a row with the Head, I jolly well don't! I'm getting out of sight. I say, give me a bunk up!"

Bunter scrambled up a gnarled old oak, of which the branches jutted right across the footpath. Wharton gave a sniff, and Johnny Bull a grunt, but Bob Cherry gave the fat Owl a bunk, and Bunter clambered into the leafy tree. He gasped and gurgled as he clambered, and Bob was rewarded for his aid by a foot clumping on his chin, which caused him to utter a startled yelp.

"Ow!"

The bobbing hat was seen to turn in the direction of the juniors. The wearer thereof had heard them.

Bunter, at least, was in safe cover as Sir Hilton Popper came striding out into the footpath. He had reached a thick bough that jutted over the path, and lay along it, holding on to jutting twigs.

Had Sir Hilton looked up, no doubt he would have spotted the fat figure sprawling on the branch, and the uneasy eyes blinking down through the big spectacles.

But Sir Hilton Popper did not look up. He strode out into the footpath, and halted in front of the group of juniors, right under Bunter's bough. The fat junior could have touched the top of his hat by stretching down his hand.

Bunter Drops In!

"HATS off!" murmured Bob Cherry.

Five fellows raised their hats very politely to the lord of Popper Court. The Famous Five did not, as a matter of fact, think very much of Sir Hilton Popper, Baronet. They regarded him as crusty-tempered, overbearing, and rather an old ass! Still, he was a governor of the school, and, anyhow, he was an elderly man, and respect was due to age. So they "capped" him politely.

Sir Hilton stared at them, his grizzled brow wrinkled over his gleaming eyeglass. He had a gun under his arm. No doubt he had been at his favourite entertainment of killing some of his hapless feathered or furry fellow-creatures.

"Huh!" he grunted.

Nobody could have supposed that he was glad to see the schoolboys there. But he did not look so crusty as usual. He did not order them off the path, and out of the woods. He glared at them through his eyeglass, and grunted.

"Nice afternoon, sir!" ventured Bob.

"If you have been disturbing my birds——" grunted Sir Hilton.

"The disturbfulness has not been terrific, honoured sahib!" said Hurree Jamset Ram Singh solemnly.

"Good gad!" said Sir Hilton, staring at the dusky nabob of Bhanipur. He had seen Hurree Singh more than once before, and no doubt remembered him by his remarkable variety of the English language. "You are Greyfriars boys?"

"Yes, Sir Hilton!" said Harry, repressing a grin.

Sir Hilton had met the Famous Five at least a dozen times, but, no doubt, they were very small fry in his lordly eyes, and he did not take the trouble of remembering them.

"What are you doing here?"

"Walking!" said Johnny Bull, with a grunt as expressive as Sir Hilton's own.

"Going down to the river, sir!" said Bob hastily.

"Wandering in the woods, climbing trees, and disturbing my birds, I have no doubt!" snapped Sir Hilton.

"Not at all, sir!" said Harry politely. "We haven't wandered in the woods, we haven't climbed trees, and——"

"Don't be impertinent!"

The Famous Five smiled. They could see that Sir Hilton Popper, for some unknown reason, was suppressing his irritable temper.

Billy Bunter, on the branch above, suppressed his breathing. The reference to climbing trees alarmed Bunter. Bunter had climbed that oak. He had, by his excessive caution, put himself in the wrong. He was the least likely of the party to pull through without a row, if the lord of Popper Court spotted him. So he was more anxious than ever not to be spotted. The footpath was the public's. The trees were Sir Hilton's. Bunter was a trespasser, though the Famous Five were not.

"You are Greyfriars boys," went on Sir Hilton. "Is one of you named Coker?"

"Coker!" repeated Harry Wharton blankly.

Coker of the Fifth was at least six inches taller than any of the juniors. He was a Fifth Form senior, and they were Lower boys. Sir Hilton's question showed that he was quite unacquainted with Horace Coker, though evidently he knew that great man's name.

"Yes, Coker!" rapped Sir Hilton. "If one of you is Coker I am very glad to see him—very glad! Which is it?"

It could hardly be doubted that Sir Hilton Popper must have seen Coker of the Fifth more than once. But, clearly, he did not remember him. He stared questioningly at the smiling juniors.

"Oh, no, sir!" said Harry. "Coker's a senior—a big chap——"

"Huh!" grunted Sir Hilton.

But the juniors guessed now why the lord of Popper Court was suppressing his crustiness.

Had one of this little party been Coker, no doubt Sir Hilton would have given him a gracious grin, even a grip of a bony, knuckly hand; he might even have asked him up to the house to tea!

Coker was missing something!

There was a rustle on the bough over Sir Hilton's head. The juniors were careful not to look up—they wondered uneasily whether Sir Hilton would do so. That ass Bunter was shifting!

It was Bunter's cue to be silent as the tomb. But it was not really Bunter's fault. A tree-beetle was crawling into Bunter's neck.

The fat junior could not venture to let go his hold, to deal with that beetle. He wriggled his fat neck frantically. The insect seemed all legs; and all the legs were tickling Bunter's fat neck. Leaves and twigs rustled as Bunter wriggled.

Luckily, Sir Hilton did not look up. If he noticed the rustle overhead, he put it down to the wind.

"I should be glad to see Coker!" grunted Sir Hilton. "He has done me a great service—a very great service. He must have been trespassing upon my island when he found the plunder hidden there by that rascal—huh! But I shall not hold that against him. I shall not complain to Dr. Locke on that account."

Sir Hilton evidently regarded this as a great and gracious concession.

"In fact," said Sir Hilton, "I desire to see Coker! You may take him a message—no, no; probably foolish schoolboys would forget all about it."

"Thank you, sir," said Bob meekly.

And the foolish schoolboys grinned.

"I shall telephone," said Sir Hilton. "Who is his Form-master? What is his name?"

"Coker's in the Fifth, sir. Prout's his Form-master."

"Prout! Prout!" repeated Sir Hilton. "I think I remember the name. Very good."

As Sir Hilton had asked Mr. Prout to dinner at least once in that term, he contrived to remember the name!

"Very good," he repeated. "Prout—yes, yes, Prout! Very good! You may go! Go straight on your way—I will not allow wandering in my woods—disturbing my birds. By gad, if I find that you have been climbing trees, I will lay my stick about you."

"You're awfully good, sir!" said Bob.

"The goodfulness is terrific!"

"What—what?" barked Sir Hilton. "Don't answer me back! Go! Go at once!"

The Famous Five shifted uneasily.

Bunter—owing to his excessive caution—was unable to move a limb! Bunter was perched on the branch over Sir Hilton's hat!

Sir Hilton Popper stood where he was, staring grimly after the juniors as they went. Perhaps he suspected them of intending to wander in the woods, or climb trees, if his lordly back was turned.

From above, two exasperated eyes glared at Sir Hilton through a big pair of spectacles.

Bunter wondered if the beast was ever going!

The beetle, by that time, had crawled right inside Billy Bunter's collar, and was nestling down comfortably in the small of his back.

It felt horrid.

Bunter gave convulsive jerks and wriggles. He was

94

not well up in natural history, and did not know whether beetles bit or not. But he was in momentary expectation of a sharp nip.

Meanwhile, the tickling of his podgy back was getting unendurable. He wriggled and wriggled.

Harry Wharton & Co. moved slowly towards the path that led through the wood towards the river. Then Sir Hilton grunted and moved.

He was going at last!

Unfortunately, it was at that moment that the tormented Owl of the Remove reached the limit of endurance.

Risky as it was, Bunter released one fat hand, to smack at that beetle.

He smacked—slipped—and rolled. The next second he was off the branch.

A horrified squeak escaped Bunter as he felt himself going. Before that squeak was fairly uttered he was gone!

Crash!

Sir Hilton Popper did not know what was happening. He had a vague impression that an uprooted oak-tree was crashing on his head.

He gave a gurgling gasp, and collapsed under the crash.

Bunter rolled off him.

"Urrrrggh!" gurgled Sir Hilton.

"Oooogh!" spluttered Bunter.

Bunter sat up dizzily.

Sir Hilton Popper sat up, clutching at his hat.

Bunter bounded to his feet.

For the moment Sir Hilton Popper was completely blindfolded by the hat. He could not see Bunter. But that happy state of affairs was not likely to last long.

So long as it lasted Bunter had a chance! He bounded up—and he bounded away! He flew!

He vanished!

He did not keep to the path. He plunged headlong through the wood, only anxious to escape being seen, regardless of disturbing birds. Fluttering and cackling accompanied his wild flight! Birds were disturbed on all sides—a most awful offence! Regardless, Bunter bolted on.

Sir Hilton, sitting in the path, struggled with his hat. He wrenched at that hat. He wrestled with it. He got it off at last. He staggered to his feet, in a dizzy state, crimson with wrath.

It was not the oak that had fallen on his head! He knew what it must have been—a young rascal hiding in the tree! The sounds that followed Bunter's flight told him all. Gasping, he plunged in pursuit—as reckless as Bunter of disturbed birds!

But he had no chance.

Bunter, whose motions generally resembled those of a tired snail, was now putting up a speed worthy of a wild, untamed zebra. Leaving an alarmed bird population fluttering and cackling behind him, Billy Bunter got out of Popper Court woods, into the lane, and ran—and ran —and ran!

Sir Hilton was left with nothing but a smashed hat to remind him of the episode. Which was very fortunate for Bunter, for had the baronet's grasp closed on him, there was little doubt that Bunter's state would have resembled that of Sir Hilton's hat!

Peter Todd picked up a cricket-stump and stepped to the doorway of Study No. 7 in the Remove. He was only just in time. Bolsover major, about to rush in, jumped back from the business-end of the stump.

"Kik-kik-keep him out, Toddy!" gasped Billy Bunter.

Billy Bunter was in the armchair in his study. Ever since his wild adventure in Popper Court woods Bunter had been taking a rest—a much-needed rest.

But though Billy Bunter's fat person was at rest in the armchair, his mind was far from being at rest. He was sure—almost sure—that Sir Hilton Popper had not spotted him in the wood, with the crunched hat over his eyes. But he would have preferred to be quite, quite sure.

If nothing were heard from Popper Court, it was all right! But Bunter had to wait, to learn whether anything was going to be heard. It was an anxious period of waiting.

Meanwhile, he had another worry, nearer home. Bolsover major, by that time, had recovered more or less from the terrific whopping Coker had given him in his study. But if Bolsover was feeling better, it was absolutely certain that his temper would be no better—but worse. Bunter was not surprised when the bully of the Remove arrived at Study No. 7. He was not surprised to see a fives bat in his hand. But he was deeply alarmed.

Luckily, Peter was a fighting-man, if Bunter was not. Nobody was going to throw his weight about in Toddy's study. It was another respite.

"Hook it," said Peter amicably.

"Gerrout of the way!" roared Bolsover major. "I'm going to smash that fat rotter! Do you hear?"

"Quite!" assented Peter. "I think all Greyfriars can hear, old bean."

All the Remove could, at all events. Fellows came out of the other studies. Harry Wharton came along from Study No. 1, with a frown on his face. Percy Bolsover had his good points; but he was a good deal of a bully; and it was not uncommon for the captain of the Remove to have trouble with him on that account. Head boy of a Form had duties to do—and one of them was to see that fellows like Bolsover did not take undue advantage of their size and weight.

"I'll smash you first, Peter Todd, if you like!" bawled Bolsover. "Let me get at that fat rotter, will you?"

He barged into the doorway again. Peter lunged with the stump. It took effect on Bolsover's waistcoat, and the burly Removite jumped back again, with a yell.

"Sorry!" said Peter politely. "But you can't barge in here, old bean."

"What on earth's the row?" asked Vernon-Smith.

"Chuck it, Bolsover!" said Redwing.

Bolsover major did not heed. He jumped at Peter Todd, and the fives bat crashed on the cricket-stump.

"Oh, crikey!" gasped Bunter, his eyes almost bulging through his spectacles, as he blinked at the fencing match in the doorway of Study No. 7.

E

Crash! Crash! Bang! Clatter!

The cricket-stump had the best of it. The fives bat went whirling in the air, and once more Bolsover major backed away from a poke in the waistcoat.

Harry Wharton caught the bat as it whirled.

"Give me that bat!" howled Bolsover.

The captain of the Remove put it behind him.

"You don't want this," he remarked.

"I'll jolly well take it, if you don't hand it over!"

"If you do, you'll take it on your bags, hard!" retorted Wharton. "You've been batted for bullying before, Bolsover, and if you ask for it, there's plenty more on tap!"

"Hear, hear!" grinned Bob Cherry.

"I say, you fellows," squeaked Bunter, "keep him off! I haven't done anything. It wasn't my fault Coker thrashed him——"

Bolsover major clenched his big fists. Wharton was a sturdy fellow, but the burly Bolsover almost towered over him. But the captain of the Remove faced him quietly.

"Chuck it!" he said. "If Bunter's done anything—I dare say he has—give it a name! But you're not pitching into him with a bat!"

"He pinched toffee from my study this afternoon!"

"I didn't!" howled Bunter.

"You jolly well did!" said Harry Wharton. "If there was any toffee there, you pinched it, if you could get your paws on it!"

"Oh, really, Wharton——"

"We can take Bolsover's word for that!" went on the captain of the Remove.

"What about my word?" howled Bunter.

"Ha, ha, ha!"

"I never had the toffee! I never went to the study!" howled Bunter. "You can ask Dupont—he was there and saw me——"

"Ha, ha, ha!"

"Bunter had the toffee," said the captain of the Remove. "Shut up, Bunter! But Bunter scrounges tuck from every

tudy in the Remove, without fellows raising Cain about
t. I dare say Bunter could tell me what became of a bag
f bullseyes I left in my study this morning."

"I don't know anything about your rotten bullseyes,"
oared Bunter indignantly. "I never saw them, and never
ouched them. There were only about a dozen, too."

"Ha, ha, ha!"

"Bunter ought to be whopped for grub-raiding," went
on the captain of the Remove. "A fellow's entitled to
hat."

"Beast!"

"Leave me alone, then!" hooted Bolsover major.

Wharton shook his head.

"You look like overdoing it," he answered. "You can
give Bunter one whop if you like—and I'll see you do it!
Stop at that!"

"I'm going to smash him!"

"Exactly what you're not going to do!" said the cap-
ain of the Remove coolly. "You're not going to bully
anybody, Bolsover—especially a fat rabbit who can't
put his hands up."

"I tell you——" roared Bolsover.

"Oh, chuck it!" said Ogilvy. "Bunter's had toffee out
of my study, without the roof being raised about it."

"'Tain't the toffee, you silly ass! I don't care twopence
about the toffee! I've been pounded nearly to a pancake
by that idiot Coker——"

"Well, Bunter's not responsible for Coker's actions,"
said Peter Todd. "Why, he's hardly responsible for his
own."

"Ha, ha, ha!"

"He scuttled into Coker's study with me after him!"
hooted Bolsover. "He put it into Coker's head that I'd
come there to whop him, and that howling ass pitched
into me, thinking so——"

"Ha, ha, ha!" yelled the fellows in the Remove passage.

"And that fat villain got away while Coker was whopping me!" howled Bolsover major. "That was why he
pulled the idiot's leg——"

"Ha, ha, ha!"

"You can cackle!" roared the enraged Bolsover. "But I'm going to smash him for it!"

"Now chuck it!" said the captain of the Remove.

"I'll smash the lot of you!"

"Will you chuck it?"

"No!" roared Bolsover major.

"Frog's-march!" said the captain of the Remove.

Bolsover major wished, perhaps, that he had "chucked" it when his arms and legs were grasped, and he was taken up the passage in the frog's-march. By the time he reached his own study, Study No. 10, he was shrieking to the juniors to let go. They let go, in the doorway of Study No. 10—spinning Bolsover major headlong in, and sending him sprawling at the feet of Dupont, his astonished study-mate.

"Now take a rest, old man!" said Bob Cherry. "Lots more if you want it—but why ask for it, if you dont?"

And the door was slammed on the bully of the Remove, and he was left to gurgle for his second wind.

Apparently he decided to take Bob's advice—and a rest—for the door did not reopen.

The crowd in the passage broke up, grinning. And in Study No. 7, Billy Bunter was grinning, too. Danger was over—for the time, at least—and Billy Bunter seemed rather amused to see Peter rubbing his nose, from which a crimson stream exuded.

"Bother that fathead!" grunted Peter. "I shall have a prize boko for days—— Ow!"

"He, he, he!"

Peter glared at the fat Owl.

"Do you think that's funny?" he bawled.

"Well, it looks funny!" grinned Bunter. "Bit like a squashed strawberry, old chap! He, he, he!"

Peter breathed hard and deep. A nose that looked a twin to a squashed strawberry was, perhaps, funny, from a spectator's point of view—but there was nothing funny in it to the owner. And as that nose had been punched n Bunter's defence, the fat Owl's amusement really was a little misplaced.

"It won't spoil your good looks, old chap!" said Bunter.

"Won't it?" grinned Peter.

"No! You see, you haven't any."

Peter breathed harder and deeper. He did not answer in words; but he looked about the study, for the cricket-stump that had flown from his hand. He found it and picked it up.

"What do you want that for, now?" asked Bunter.

"I don't want it!" answered Toddy. "You do!"

"Eh! I don't!" said Bunter, in surprise.

"You do—and you're getting it!"

The next moment, Bunter discovered what the stump was wanted for. It landed with a swipe, and the fat Owl bounded for the door. It landed again as he scuttled into the passage.

"Ow! Beast!" roared Bunter, as he fled.

"Come back and have another!" hooted Peter, brandishing the stump in the study doorway.

"Beast!"

Bunter did not come back. He accelerated and vanished!

A Rag in The Fifth!

HORACE COKER grinned.

It was the following day, and, after class, Coker was walking down to the gates with Potter and Greene.

He grinned as he passed Bolsover major of the Remove in the quad.

Bolsover gave Coker the blackest of black looks. Even after the lapse of twenty-four hours, Bolsover was still feeling twinges from that terrific whopping in Coker's study. In response to his black look, Coker gave him a cheery grin.

"Want some more?" he queried banteringly.

"Oh, come on, Coker!" said Potter. "We don't want to be late for the pictures."

"Bother that fag," said Greene. "Come on!"

"Don't jaw!" said Coker.

However, he came on; and Bolsover major scowled after the three as they went out of gates.

He scowled thoughtfully.

Coker & Co., it seemed, were going to the pictures at Courtfield. That meant that Coker would not be back for a long time—probably not much before calling-over.

There was senior cricket practice going on, on Big Side; and most of the other members of the Fifth were there.

Bolsover's eyes gleamed.

He had been waiting for a chance to "get back" on Coker! This looked like a chance! Bolsover was thinking of a rag in Coker's study. He could not rag the hefty Horace, as he would have liked to do. But he could rag his study—when he was absent!

It was, indeed, as good a chance as he could have desired. The coast was absolutely clear. Coker & Co. were off the scene—most, if not all, of the Fifth were away from the studies—and Mr. Prout, the Fifth Form master, had gone off for a walk with Mr. Quelch after class— which meant that both Coker's Form-master and Bolsover's Form-master were safe out of the way. Bolsover thought it over for a few minutes, and made up his mind.

But he did not start immediately for the Fifth Form studies. He glanced round and called to some Remove fellows.

"Seen Bunter?"

"Oh, leave Bunter alone!" answered Harry Wharton. 'Do you want another frog's-march, fathead?"

Since that frog's-march Bolsover major had given Bunter no attention—much to the fat Owl's relief. But the bully of the Remove was not the man to forget the matter.

"Can't a fellow speak to a chap?" he snapped. "I want to speak to the fat chump. I'm not going to lick him."

"Oh, all right! Better look in the tuckshop, if you want him."

"He's there, if he's got any money," remarked Bob Cherry. "If he hasn't, he's trying to borrow some off Mauly. If you draw the tuckshop blank, look for Lord Mauleverer."

Bolsover major stalked away, leaving the chums of the Remove laughing. He found the fat Owl of the Remove blinking in at the window of the school shop.

Bunter eyed him warily through his big spectacles as he came up. But he was comforted by the sight of the Famous Five in the offing.

Bolsover did not look hostile.

"Oh, here you are!" he said. "Did you know Coker had gone out?"

"No; has he?"

"He's left a hamper in his study."

"Oh!" said Bunter.

"Serve him jolly well right to snaffle it!" said Bolsover.

"Oh, really, Bolsover! I hope I'm not the fellow to snaffle a fellow's tuck."

"You silly fathead!" grunted Bolsover major, and he went into the tuckshop, leaving Bunter to his own devices.

Billy Bunter rolled off towards the House.

Bunter reached the landing at the end of the Fifth Form passage, and was blinking cautiously along that passage through his big spectacles.

Billy Bunter was not a bright youth. But he was bright enough to be on his guard on this occasion. Very likely, of course, Bolsover would be glad to see Coker's hamper snaffled, in revenge for that whopping. More likely still, however, he would be glad to land Bunter in Coker's clutches.

If a hamper was there, and Coker wasn't, Bunter was not the fellow to let his chances, like the sunbeams, pass him by. But he was fearfully cautious. For several minutes he blinked along a deserted passage. Then he rolled up the passage to Coker's study.

If Horace was there, it was, after all, easy enough to ascertain the fact, and scoot before Coker could buzz a Latin grammar at his head. If he was not, it was all serene.

Bunter tapped!

As there was no reply, he opened the door and blinked in. The study was empty.

Bunter rolled in and shut the door.

Then he blinked round for the hamper. Only too well Bunter knew what gorgeous hampers Coker sometimes received from his affectionate Aunt Judy. He had sampled the contents of more than one of them.

But there was no hamper to be seen now. Bunter looked in the study cupboard—he looked under the table; he blinked behind the screen in the corner. No hamper rewarded his search.

"Beast!" hissed Bunter.

Evidently, Bolsover major had been pulling his fat leg.

The door opened suddenly.

Bunter spun round, with a squeak of alarm. He expected to see Coker. But it was Bolsover major who entered.

He stepped in quickly, shut the door, and turned the key in the lock.

"Here we are again!" said Bolsover agreeably.

"I—I say——" stammered Bunter, backing round the table. "I—I say, you touch me, you beast, and I'll jolly well yell."

"Who's going to touch you?" inquired Bolsover blandly.

"Oh!" ejaculated Bunter. "What did you pull my leg for, you beast? You jolly well wanted to get me here— I can see that now——"

"What a brain!" said Bolsover.

"Well, I'm jolly well going——" Bunter made a move towards the door. The bully of the Remove pulled the key out of the lock.

"You're not going till you've done what you came here to do, old fat bean," said Bolsover major pleasantly.

"There isn't any hamper——"

"Never mind that! You came here to rag this study."

"I didn't!" gasped Bunter.

"You did!" answered Bolsover major coolly. "And I'm going to sit on the table and watch you do it. Plenty of time—Prout's out, and the Fifth are at cricket, and Coker's gone to the pictures with his pals. Still, you may as well get going."

"You silly ass!" gasped Bunter in great alarm. "I'm not going to rag a Fifth Form study! There would be an awful row."

"There will be a row if you don't!" said Bolsover still blandly. "You're going to rag this study till it looks as if a cyclone had struck it. You got me a fearful whopping from Coker yesterday. Now you can earn one for yourself. I shan't give you away, of course; but if Coker finds out who ragged his study, I fancy you will get toco. You can take the chance."

"Look here, if you want the study ragged, you can jolly well rag it yourself," gasped Bunter. "I'm not having a hand in it."

"You are—two hands, in fact!" declared Bolsover major. "I advise you to get going. I'm not going to rag the study—but I'm going to pelt you with Coker's books till you begin."

"I—I say—yoop!" spluttered Bunter as the bully of the Remove picked up a Latin grammar and buzzed it. It caught Bunter under the chin, and caused him to sit down on Coker's carpet with a sudden bump.

"Oh, here's Coker's compasses!" remarked Bolsover major. He picked them up. "Just the thing for you, Bunter! If you want to be punctured——"

Bunter squirmed wildly away.

"Ow! Keep off, you beast! I—I'll rag the study if

105

you like—keep those compasses away—— **Yow-ow-ow!**"

Bolsover major grinned and sat on the corner of the study table, compasses in hand. Billy Bunter cast a longing blink at the door. But the door was locked, and the key in Bolsover's pocket. There was no escape for the hapless fat Owl.

His remarkable strategy of the previous day had not yet been paid for—but now it had to be paid for with interest.

"I—I say, suppose somebody comes to the study!" stammered Bunter. "We—we shall got copped here, old chap! I—I shouldn't mind but—but I don't want to get you into a row."

"Get on with it!"

"I mean you clear off, old fellow, and—and leave me to it—— Yarooh! Keep those compasses away, you beast! Wow!"

"Have another?" grinned Bolsover.

"I—I say—— Oh! Keep off! I'm going it, ain't I?" howled Bunter—and he went it!

There was no help for it; it was either ragging Coker's study, or taking a series of jabs from Coker's compasses. Bunter did not want to rag the study, but still less did he want to be jabbed by the compasses.

So he set to work. Bolsover major sat on the table, grinning, and watched him. Every now and then he spurred the fat Owl on with a flourish of the compasses. Bunter was not keen to rag, but he was very keen to get through and escape from those dangerous quarters, so he put his beef into it.

Books and papers flew all over the study; the fender was overturned, the mantelpiece swept clear over it; bookshelves were emptied, and ink splashed over the books, the carpet, and the furniture. Coker's study soon had a fearfully dishevelled appearance.

"I—I say, that'll do!" gasped Bunter.

"My dear chap, you haven't started yet!" said Bolsover major genially. "If you want these compasses——"

"Ow! Beast! Keep off!"

106

"Ow! Beast!" groaned the fat Removite, "keep off!"

Billy Bunter re-started. He strewed Coker's crockery-ware over the floor among the books and papers and ink; he jerked down pictures, and overturned chairs amid the general havoc. Then he paused for breath.

"I say——"

Bolsover major held up his hand in warning; there was a footstep in the passage outside.

"Oh, crikey!" breathed Bunter.

He felt quite dizzy at the thought of Coker coming back and finding him in the study, and the study in that awful state.

Tap!

Billy Bunter gave a gasp of relief. Clearly it was not Coker coming back; he would not have tapped at the door of his own study.

The door-handle turned.

Having tapped, the newcomer was going to open the door—and would have done so the next moment had it not been locked.

But the door, being locked, did not open. There came another tap on the panels.

"Oh, lor'!" breathed Bunter.

"Better answer him," whispered Bolsover major. "Tell the silly idiot to go away, whoever he is!"

"Master Coker, sir!" came a surprised voice through the door. It was the voice of Trotter, the House page, and he was surprised at finding the study door locked. "You in there, sir? You're wanted!"

"Oh, crikey!" breathed Bunter.

Trotter waited for an answer. He had no doubt, of course, that one, at least, of the owners of the study was there as the door was locked inside—Coker, or Potter, or Greene. It was Coker he had come for. Horace Coker, it seemed, was wanted—at a very unlucky moment for the two juniors who were busy in the study.

Bolsover major made the fat Owl a threatening gesture.

"Master Coker, sir!" called Trotter. "Please open the door, sir!"

Billy Bunter gave a fat little cough. That was his usual preliminary to ventriloquial stunts.

That was, after all, easy to the Greyfriars ventriloquist. Billy Bunter could imitate any voice he knew, especially if it was a little out of the common—as Coker's gruff bark certainly was.

"Go it, you fat idiot!" whispered Bolsover. He was uneasy now. He did not want Trotter to go and mention that Coker's study was locked and that there was somebody in it who refused to answer.

Tap, tap!

"Master Coker, sir!" came Trotter's voice. "Please open the door, sir! It's me, sir—Trotter!"

"Oh, don't bother!" said Bunter, with so startling an imitation of the gruff tones of Horace Coker that it made Bolsover jump, though he was expecting it.

"It's a message, sir!" came Trotter's answer.

"I'm sporting my oak, bother you!" grunted Coker's voice from the mouth of the Greyfriars ventriloquist. "I'm not letting anybody in. I've got a dashed exercise to finish for Prout. What the thump do you want?"

"Shall I tell you through the keyhole, sir?" asked Trotter, more and more surprised.

It was not uncommon for a fellow with work on hand to "sport his oak." But it was rather uncommon with Coker, who was not of a studious nature. Still, if Coker chose to sport his oak, that was no business of Trotter's.

"Yes—and cut it short!" growled the gruff voice within.

"Sir Hilton Popper, sir——"

"Wha-a-at?"

"On the telephone, sir——"

"Oh!" gasped Bunter.

"He wants to speak to you, sir."

"Oh!"

"He rang up, sir, on Mr. Prout's telephone," said Trotter, through the keyhole. "Mr. Prout being out, sir, I took the call; and Sir Hilton Popper says, sir—he says that he wants to speak to you, sir."

"Oh, all right!"

"I didn't know whether you was indoors, sir, so I told Sir Hilton Popper, sir, I'd see," went on Trotter. "So he said he'd ring off, sir, and you was to ring up immegit."

Billy Bunter grunted.

This was about the last thing he would have expected to hear. The lord of Popper Court, being a governor of the school, might have rung up the Head on the telephone, but, so far as Bunter knew, he had never rung up a Greyfriars fellow before.

It was very annoying—to Bunter.

But he remembered what he had heard the baronet saying to the Famous Five in Popper Court woods the previous day.

Sir Hilton had said that he would telephone, and no doubt he had rung up Mr. Prout to ask to speak to Coker, who had rendered him that great service in recovering the snaffled silver. Prout being out, the call had been taken for him by the House page, and Sir Hilton told him to send Coker to the phone.

It was quite simple—but very irritating at the moment. Fortunately, Trotter had no doubt that it was Coker who was answering him from within the study.

"Sir Hilton Popper said he would wait, sir," went on Trotter. "P'r'aps you'll go and ring up on Mr. Prout's phone, sir? He said immegit! "

"Oh, all right! " answered Bunter in Coker's voice, and he was greatly relieved to hear Trotter's footsteps die away down the passage.

Bolsover major chuckled when the page was gone.

"Lucky I locked the door," he remarked. "If that young ass had got a squint inside it would have been all over the shop by the time Coker comes in."

"Oh, crikey! " said Bunter.

He blinked round the wrecked study. The havoc there was quite amusing to Bolsover major, but it was deeply alarming to the Owl of the Remove. He felt quite dizzy at the thought of Horace Coker discovering who had dealt with his quarters like that.

"Get on with it! " said Bolsover.

"I—I say, we—we'd better clear!" gasped Bunter. "I—I think we'd better get out of this, Bolsover!"

"Think again!" suggested Bolsover.

"I—I say, that old ass will be ringing up again if he doesn't get an answer from Coker. We shall have Trotter up here again."

"Oh!" said Bolsover. He realised that the argument was good. If Sir Hilton Popper was waiting for Coker's call, so impatient and autocratic an old gentleman was not likely to wait long.

"Let's get out!" urged Bunter. "If Trotter comes up again, and spots us going, Coker will know who ragged his study, and——"

"That won't hurt me," grinned Bolsover. "I haven't done any ragging."

"Beast!" hissed Bunter.

"Trotter will be up here again in ten minutes or so, when that old ass Popper rings up again. It won't take him long to find out that Coker's out of gates, and has been out for an hour. He will jolly well know it wasn't Coker answered him. Your jolly old ventriloquism's pretty well known, Bunter."

"Oh!" gasped Bunter.

"You've played tricks on Trotter with it before now— making the House dame call him, and that sort of thing!" chuckled Bolsover. "Bet you Trotter will tumble. If he mentions it to Coker——"

"Oh, crikey!"

"Pack some exercise-books in your bags before Coker comes back," said Bolsover major, with a roar of laughter. "Ha, ha, ha!"

"You—you—you beast!" gasped Bunter, in utter dismay. "You—you awful beast! You've jolly well landed me now!"

"Didn't you land me yesterday?" grinned Bolsover.

"Oh lor'! I—I say, old chap—I—I say, you go and give old Popper that call he's expecting, and shoo him off!" gasped Bunter.

"I'll watch it!"

"You can do it, old chap! Popper wouldn't know your voice," said Bunter eagerly. "He doesn't know Coker at all—I heard him ask some Remove chaps yesterday if one of them was Coker. Safe as houses."

"Quite safe?" asked Bolsover.

"Perfectly safe."

"Then you go and do it!" grinned Bolsover major.

"Oh, really, Bolsover——"

"Ha, ha, ha!"

Bolsover major unlocked the door, and left the study. Billy Bunter rolled out after him. Both of them hurriedly left the precincts of the Fifth—Bolsover grinning with satisfaction; Bunter wriggling with dismay and apprehension.

Bolsover strolled out into the quad, grinning. Billy Bunter rolled away to Prout's study. Any minute now, Sir Hilton Popper might ring up again, and Sir Hilton had to be barred off while there was yet time. Billy Bunter, in great haste, rolled into the Fifth Form master's study, shut the door, picked up the receiver, and gave the number of Popper Court on the telephone.

"Huh!"

That sound, something between a grunt and a snort, announced that Sir Hilton Popper was on the telephone, in the library at Popper Court.

Billy Bunter quaked.

Sir Hilton was a terrifying old gentleman, and Bunter could not forget that he had fallen from a branch, on Sir Hilton's hat the day before.

Still, there really was no danger. It was not even necessary for Bunter to use his ventriloquial trickery. Sir Hilton's remarks the day before showed that he knew nothing about Coker. If he did not know Coker by sight, certainly he was not likely to know his voice.

"Huh! What? What? Who is speaking? Is that Coker?"

"Yes!" gasped Bunter.

"Oh! Coker!" The bark over the wires became a little more genial. "Oh! I am glad to speak to you, Coker!"

112

"I—I came at—at once, sir——"

"Very good! Quite so! I am much obliged to you, Coker! I understand, from your headmaster, that it was you, Coker, who recovered the articles stolen from my house last week by the man Leech——"

"Oh! Yes, sir!"

"You were trespassing on the island in the river at the time——" The bark became less genial.

"Oh! No! I haven't been anywhere near the island——"

"What—what?"

"I—I mean——"

"Nonsense! I am not angry with you, my boy! The rascal concealed his plunder on the island, and you found it there. You must have been trespassing. But I overlook it—I overlook it!"

"Oh! Yes, sir! Thank you!" gasped Bunter. "Is—is that all, sir! I—I think somebody's calling me——"

"I am not finished yet!"

"Oh, lor'!"

"What—what did you say, Coker?"

"I—I said pip-pip-please go on, sir!" groaned Bunter.

Bunter was only anxious to get through, and get out of such dangerous quarters as a senior Form-master's study. All Bunter wanted to do was to "shoo" the baronet off, like a troublesome chicken.

But it was impossible to cut off till Sir Hilton had finished. Sir Hilton, at present, had no suspicion that it was not Coker speaking. Bunter did not want to make him suspicious. Very much he did not.

"Now, my boy"—the bark was genial again—"I am under a very great obligation to you. I feel that I am bound to acknowledge it in some way."

"Oh!" gasped Bunter.

"I shall excuse you for trespassing on my island. I have told your headmaster so. But I desire to see you."

"Oh!" gasped Bunter again.

"To-morrow, I think, is a half-holiday at the school——"

"Yes, sir, Wednesday——"

"Come and see me at Popper Court."

"Oh!"

"I shall be glad to see you, Coker, and make your acquaintance."

"Ah!"

"You will take tea with me——"

"Um!"

"What did you say, Coker?"

"I—I shall be pip-pip——"

"What?"

"Pip-pip-pleased, sir!" gasped Bunter.

"Very good! Now," went on Sir Hilton, more and more genial, "I am not—hum—accustomed to entertaining schoolboys—hum! But I have been a schoolboy myself —hum—a long time ago, by gad! I shall try to make you enjoy your visit! The fat of the land, what?"

"Oh, crikey!" breathed Bunter. Sir Hilton Popper, trying hard to be genial, struck him rather as a tiger trying to purr like a cat!

"You have placed me under an obligation, Coker! I shall acknowledge it—recognise it! I shall be delighted to meet you, Coker!"

Bunter blinked at the telephone. He rather wished that he was Coker. He would have shared Sir Hilton's delight, with tea at Popper Court, and the fat of the land. All the more, because his celebrated postal order had not yet arrived, and he was, as usual, stony. It was a delightful vision—if only he had been Coker, instead of merely spoofing on the telephone in Coker's name.

"Tea on the lawn at four!" said Sir Hilton. "I shall endeavour—hum—to make it one that a schoolboy may enjoy. Sticky things—hum! You may bring some friends, if you desire. Tennis—badminton—what?"

"Oh!" gasped Bunter.

Sir Hilton was making an effort. That was perceptible. He did not like boyish company, and he would have enjoyed nothing less than a schoolboy party. But he was under an obligation to Coker of the Fifth, and he was

114

going to acknowledge it. Doubtless Sir Hilton considered that an invitation to Popper Court, and his own lofty and lordly presence, was a sufficient reward for any service, however great.

"Come early," went on Sir Hilton, evidently determined to go the whole hog while he was about it. "Say three," he added rather hastily, as if struck by a sudden dread that Coker might make it two, or even one!

"Oh! Yes, sir!"

"Very well! I shall expect you at—at three, Coker! Bring two or three friends if you like—three or four!" added Sir Hilton, with another perceptible effort. "It is settled—what?"

"Oh! Yes! Thank you, sir!" gasped Bunter.

"Not at all—not at all! Good-bye, Coker!"

"Gig-gig-good-bye, sir!"

Sir Hilton Popper rang off.

Billy Bunter put up Mr. Prout's receiver, and stood blinking at the telephone in blank dismay.

He had "shoo'd" the baronet off. That was all right. There would be no ring to bring Trotter on the scene again. The havoc in Coker's study would remain undiscovered till Coker came in—hours yet. But——

But on the morrow Sir Hilton Popper would be expecting Coker at Popper Court. Tea on the lawn; the baronet, in his best temper, expecting guests—and nobody arriving! Coker, certainly, would not arrive, as Coker knew nothing whatever about it. What was going to happen then?

Angry inquiry—which would only too likely lead to Bunter! All Bunter had wanted to do was to shoo Sir Hilton off like an intrusive chicken. But Sir Hilton was no chicken, and not to be shoo'd off. He was shoo'd off till the morrow, and then——

"Oh, lor'!" groaned Bunter.

It was a worried Bunter that rolled away from Prout's study.

What About It!

"I SAY, you fellows!"

"Roll away, barrel!"

"Oh, really, Wharton, I haven't come here to tea——"

"You haven't!" agreed Wharton.

"I want to ask you fellows' advice," said Bunter.

Harry Wharton & Co. came up to Study No. 1 in the Remove in a cheery crowd after cricket practice. They were not surprised to find Billy Bunter there, as it was tea-time. But they were surprised to hear that it was advice, and not tea, of which he was in search.

"Advice!" repeated Bob Cherry.

"Yes, old chap!"

"Right as rain!" agreed Bob. "If that's it, you can look on me as your kind Uncle Robert! I advise you to wash your neck!"

"Look here, no larks, you dummies!" hooted Bunter. "I tell you, I'm in a scrape, and I want you fellows to advise me. I say, you fellows, do you think a man who didn't know me by sight might take me for a Fifth Form man?"

"Eh?"

"What?"

The Famous Five gazed at Bunter in wonder. That was an utterly unexpected and surprising question. Bunter had, at least, suceeded in riveting their attention.

"I mean, I'm rather tall for a junior, ain't I?" said Bunter, drawing himself up to his full height—which, as a matter of absolute fact, was far from impressive.

"Only sideways!" said Bob, shaking his head.

"I mean, jealousy apart!" said Bunter irritably.

"Oh, crikey!"

"Suppose you fellows saw me for the first time, and didn't know I was a Remove chap, what would you take me for?" asked Bunter anxiously.

"A barrel!" answered Bob.

"You silly ass!" shrieked Bunter. "Can't you be serious? I say, suppose I saw old Popper, think he would take me for a Fifth Form man?"

"Hardly!" said Harry Wharton, laughing. "But what the thump are you thinking of pulling old Popper's leg for, you fat ass?"

"Well, he's never seen Coker," argued Bunter. "You remember he asked you yesterday if one of you was Coker. You were an ass to tell him that Coker was a big chap, Wharton—but you always were a silly ass! It might make him suspicious if I went there as Coker."

Billy Bunter's powerful intellect had been at work, evidently, since he had got off Prout's telephone. But the chums of the Remove, who knew nothing of his talk with the lord of Popper Court, could only stare at him in wonder.

"Well, you blithering ass," said Johnny Bull, "old Popper doesn't know Coker from Adam! But if you tried to spoof him like that he would jump on you at once!"

"I—I suppose it would be a risk!" muttered the fat Owl disconsolately.

"I should call it a cert!" said Frank Nugent. "But what on earth have you got in your silly nut now? If Coker's been asked to Popper Court, he's not likely to let you go instead, is he?"

"You see, he doesn't know he's been asked."

"He's been asked without knowing it?" ejaculated Bob.

"You see, I took the call——"

"Oh, my hat!"

"It's all right, as far as that goes," said Bunter. "But, you see, I'm not going to tell Coker. He would want to know how I came to take the call, and—and it might come out about his study being ragged——"

"Has Coker's study been ragged?"

"Oh, no! Not that I know of! I haven't been near the place. Besides, that beast Bolsover made me go! He stuck Coker's compasses into me till I did it. Not that I did anything, you know," added Bunter hastily. "Don't you fellows get jawing about a rag in Coker's study, and saying I did it! I don't want to have anything to do with Coker of the Fifth!"

"Ha, ha, ha!"

"You see, I'm in a bit of a scrape."

"Looks as if you are, old fat man!" said Bob. "If it's advice you want, I advise you to give up spoofing, as well as to wash your neck!"

"Oh, really, Cherry, I was fairly driven into this!" said Bunter. "That beast Bolsover made me rag Coker's study, and I should have been spotted there if I hadn't made Trotter believe Coker was at home; and then I only gave that old ass Popper a call to keep him quiet—and then he springs this on me! If I dropped in and gave Coker's name, it would be all right—if he believed I was Coker. It would keep him quiet—and there would be the tea, too! But—but he mightn't believe I was a Fifth Form man."

"The might-notfulness is terrific!" grinned Hurree Jamset Ram Singh.

And the chums of the Remove roared. Billy Bunter was not tall, even for a Lower Fourth junior. The least suspicious of baronets certainly never would have believed him to be a Fifth Form senior.

"Well, what about you, Bob?" asked Bunter.

"Eh?"

"You're the biggest chap here, and I want to keep it among my friends," said Bunter. "It will be a jolly good tea—you can rely on that. Old Popper's a bit of a beast, but he wants to be nice to Coker for getting back those tin pots and things. It's sure to be a good tea, that stands to reason. You're as tall as Price of the Fifth—a bit the start of him, I think. I say, old chap, what about it?"

"What about it?" gasped Bob Cherry. "What about my

118

going to Popper Court and calling myself by another chap's name, do you mean?"

"Yes, old fellow! You're as big as some Fifth Form men—not so big as Coker, but the old ass has never seen Coker—and you're jolly nearly as ugly, anyhow! He, he, he! What about it?"

Bob Cherry's face was a study. The expression on it as he gazed at Bunter made his friends yell.

"Ha, ha, ha!" yelled the Co.

"I say, you fellows, don't cackle! We've got to get this settled," said Bunter peevishly. "It will get me out of a row if somebody turns up as Coker and stops that old ass poking his silly nose into things! And a long-legged spindleshanks like Bob could do it——"

"The esteemed and ludicrous Bunter forgets that the absurd Sir Hilton saw Bob yesterday in the wood!" chuckled Hurree Jamset Ram Singh. "He would expect the ridiculous Bob to have been Coker yesterday if he is Coker tomorrow!"

"Ha, ha, ha!"

"Oh!" gasped Bunter. "Oh, crikey! Oh!"

"Ha, ha, ha!" yelled the Co.

Bunter gave a grunt of disgust.

"That tears it!" he said. "You won't be any good, Cherry! None of you fellows would be any good! You're too fatheaded to get by with it, anyhow, I dare say! It's a thing that requires a bit of gumption! I think I'll ask Smithy—he's got more sense than the lot of you!"

The fat Owl started for the door.

Then he turned back. He had forgotten, for the moment, that it was tea-time. But that was not a thing that Billy Bunter was likely to forget for more than a moment.

"I'll see Smithy after tea," he remarked. "If you fellows are going to have tea, I'll—— Whoop! Yoooop! Yarooooooop!"

Bob Cherry seemed to have been transfixed, for some moments. He just stood gazing at Bunter. Now, however, he woke to sudden action.

Bunter never knew what Bob kicked him for. But he

knew that Bob did kick him. Bob's boot was of too large a size to leave any doubt on that point.

"Yaroop! Beast! Yurrrooooh!" roared Bunter, bounding for the door. "I say, you fellows—— Whooop! You silly idiot—— Yow-ow-ow-woop!"

Bunter forgot tea again! Dinner, tea, and supper combined, would not have induced him to linger a moment longer. He flew.

That evening, in the Rag, there were grinning faces.

By that time, most of the Remove fellows were aware of the weird and wonderful wheeze that had germinated in the powerful intellect of William George Bunter.

Most of them thought it fearfully funny.

But few, if any, of them, had any idea of joining up, to help Bunter through. It was altogether too weird and wonderful a wheeze to recommend itself to the average fellow.

Bunter was in a scrape.

There was no doubt about it! It was well known that Coker of the Fifth, having discovered his study in a state of havoc and wreckage, was breathing wrath and vengeance on the subject. Potter and Greene, who did not always agree with Coker, agreed with him that the ragger had to be found, slaughtered, and made a horrible example of. It was their study, as well as Coker's. So they felt this as deeply as Coker.

Fortunately, there was, so far, no clue.

But was it all coming out on the morrow?

If Coker did not go to Popper Court, obviously there would be further communication—probably angry communication—from Sir Hilton! He would want to know what the dooce it meant!

Then it would come out about the spoof on the phone. Then it would come out that Trotter had gone to Coker's study to call him, and supposed that Coker had answered him—while Coker was at the pictures at Courtfield! Then all the fat would be in the fire! Ten to one, a hundred to one, it would all come home to Bunter!

Both of them would be after Bunter, if the facts came to light.

A fellow in a scrape was entitled to sympathy! Remove fellows sympathised, but they chuckled as well. Some of them would have helped Bunter out, if they could—but not to the extent of going over to Popper Court on Wednesday under the name of Coker!

Bunter tried it on, up and down the Remove, with no success. The Bounder as the most reckless fellow in the Form, might have been expected to play up. But Smithy only roared with laughter at the idea. Squiff chuckled, and Tom Brown chortled, and both refused. Peter Todd, like Bob Cherry, kicked Bunter for suggesting a trick that involved so wide a departure from the truth. Which was painful to Bunter—and very irritating, too—an absurd attention to an unimportant detail, in his opinion.

There were, at any rate, no takers.

Even the prospect of a magnificent feed was no temptation. The fact was that, apart from other considerations, it was hardly an easy matter for a Lower Fourth junior to palm himself off as a Fifth Form senior. It was altogether too risky an experiment.

Only one fellow in the Remove, in fact, was fitted by nature for playing such a part—Bolsover major, the biggest fellow in the Form, who was bigger than some fellows in the Fifth.

But as Bunter could not go near Bolsover major without danger of a kick, a cuff, or a twist of his fat ear, he had not yet put it up to Bolsover. The bully of the Remove was a last resource.

There was a chortle in the Rag when Billy Bunter rolled into that apartment after prep.

Bunter's fat face was worried; but every other face wore a grin.

By that time, most of the Remove knew about the great wheeze—fellows Bunter had asked had told other fellows, and it was getting to be the standing joke in the Form.

"I say, you fellows——" began Bunter, blinking through his big spectacles.

"Found a man yet?" chuckled the Bounder.

"I say, Smithy, you could do it——"

"Catch me going to old Popper and telling him a string of lies!" grinned Smithy.

"Well, you needn't mind that, Smithy," urged Bunter. "Look at the lies you tell Quelch!"

"Ha, ha, ha!"

"What about you, Wibley?" asked Bunter. "You're jolly clever at make-up—you could make yourself look a bit older. You're so jolly clever, you know."

William Wibley chuckled.

"A bit too clever to play the goat, old fat man!" he answered.

"I say, you fellows, where's Bolsover?"

"Are you going to ask Bolsover?" said Harry Wharton, laughing. "Guard with your left when you ask him."

"Ha, ha, ha!"

"Yah!" snorted Bunter.

Bolsover major had not yet come down from the studies, and Billy Bunter rolled away in search of him—leaving the Rag in a roar.

It was in an extremely uneasy frame of mind that the fat Owl approached Study No. 10 in the Remove.

Bunter blinked cautiously into Study No. 10. Bolsover, who was both slack and dense, had trouble with his prep, and was not through yet.

He scowled at the fat face and glimmering spectacles in his doorway, and reached for his Latin grammar.

Bunter popped back just in time.

He waited outside the study, till he heard Bolsover major slam down his books and push his chair back from the table. Then he blinked in again.

"I say, old chap!" he squeaked. "I—I say, c-can I come in?"

"Do!" said Bolsover major. "I'll jolly soon boot you out again."

"Oh, really, Bolsover——" The fat Owl eyed him uneasily through the doorway. "I—I say, old chap, it's a feed."

"Oh!" said Bolsover major more placably. "Well, if it's a feed, I'll come. You can come in, Bunter."

Bunter rolled in—hopeful. The bully of the Remove looked almost good-tempered. Music is said to soothe the savage breast; and being asked to a spread seemed to have the same effect.

"Where's the spread?" asked Bolsover. "In your study?"

"Nunno—not in my study."

"In the dorm, do you mean, after lights out?"

"Nunno—not in the dorm."

"In the Rag?"

"Nunno—not in the Rag!"

"Where the dickens is it going to be, then?" demanded Bolsover suspiciously. "If you're trying to pull my leg——"

"Oh, no, old chap! Not at all! It's a ripping spread—a topping one—really—best spread of the term——"

"Well, where's it going to be?"

"At—at Popper Court!" gasped Bunter.

Bolsover stared at him.

"At Popper Court!" he repeated. "You blithering idiot! I've heard of that rot you've been talking up and down the Remove! Is that what you've come here to talk about? By gum, I'll jolly well——"

He jumped at Bunter.

Bunter jumped at the doorway.

Bolsover major's boot reached Bunter as Bunter reached the doorway!

Thud!

"Yarooooh!"

Billy Bunter did not stop for more! Bolsover, evidently, was in no mood to listen to the voice of the charmer. Bunter's last hope was gone—and it was time for Bunter to be gone, too. He went—rapidly!

Bolsover Plays Up!

"NOT a bad idea!" said Skinner.

"Think not?" asked Bolsover major.

"Jolly good thing, if you ask me!"

"Oh!" said Bolsover thoughtfully.

It was in break the following morning.

Billy Bunter, woeful and worried, had given up hope of getting any fellow to back him up and get him out of that awful scrape by playing the part of Coker of the Fifth at Popper Court that afternoon. But it is said that the darkest hour is before dawn. There was hope for Bunter!

Bolsover major would not, probably, have listened to Bunter on the subject. But he had great respect for the judgment of Harold Skinner, who was reputed the sharpest fellow in the Remove—as well as the most unscrupulous.

"Well, look at it!" argued Skinner. "That ass, Coker, knows nothing of it, so he can't barge in. Some of the fellows say he ought to be told—but they can't tell him without giving Bunter away. That's all right. And it's safe with old Popper. He doesn't know Coker! Any man big enough to look like a Fifth Former could walk in at Popper Court this afternoon and get away with it."

"Um!" said Bolsover major.

"If I were as big as you, old chap," said Skinner, "I'd jolly well have a shot at it. Not much good my trying to make out I'm in the Fifth, though. I ain't what you'd call big, for the Remove."

Bolsover major grinned at the idea of the weedy Skinner trying to pass himself off as the brawny Coker. Still, old Popper did not know how big and brawny Coker was.

Any fellow big enough to make out that he was a senior could pull it off. Bolsover, certainly, was big enough.

"It would be a jest on that fool Coker, bagging his spread," went on Skinner. "You owe him one, Bolsover."

"That's so!" agreed Bolsover. "But——"

"And it's sure to be pretty decent," continued Skinner. "Stands to reason old Popper is jolly pleased with Coker getting back his best chromium-plated historic pots and things. He must mean to be pretty nice, or he wouldn't have asked the chap. He will do the party all right, you can depend on that. If you take it on, Bolsover, I'll back you up."

"How do you mean?" asked Bolsover.

"According to Bunter, Coker's allowed to take some friends with him. I'll come as a friend, and see you through. Snoopy would come, too, if I asked him."

Bolsover major looked thoughtful. Bagging a spread planned for Coker of the Fifth appealed to him. It would be tit for tat, in return for that whopping in Coker's study.

"By gum!" said Bolsover major. "Blessed if I don't!"

"Do!" said Skinner. "I'll come. It's safe as houses——"

"You jolly well wouldn't come if you didn't think it was!" agreed Bolsover major, with a nod.

"It's just this one occasion only—old Popper will never want to see Coker again!" said Skinner. "So it can never come out that the wrong man went."

"I don't see how it could!" agreed Bolsover.

"Good egg!" said Skinner. "The more the merrier! Even if old Popper doesn't want a crowd, he can't say anything."

"Bunter says he said three or four. We can make it five or six!" said Bolsover. "If he's laid in tuck, I don't see wasting it or leaving it for the footmen to snaffle afterwards. We'll make it a party, what?"

"It's the catch of the term!" declared Skinner. "All it wants is a big chap to play Coker, with nerve to do it—and you've got tons of nerve."

"I fancy so!" said Bolsover major.

He went away to look for Hazeldene, and Skinner to

look for Snoop. Sidney James Snoop whistled, when Skinner told him.

"Too jolly risky!" he said. "Why, old Popper would raise Cain if he found out that his leg had been pulled."

"He won't!" said Skinner. "How could he? He will never see Coker."

"He might!"

"And if he did, we're all right!" added Skinner coolly. "That fat ass, Bunter, did the spoofing—and Bolsover's going to do the rest. We are simply innocent, unsuspicious fellows who've accepted an invitation to tea."

"Oh!" said Snoop.

"If it came out," said Skinner, "Bunter would get a flogging for his telephone tricks and Bolsover another for calling himself by another chap's name. It would do them both good, if you come to that."

Snoop grinned.

"Innocent fellows like us, who simply went along to tea because a pal asked us, can't be blamed, so far as I can see," argued Skinner. "Lines, at the most, even if it comes out—and it's worth that. And it's not at all likely to come out."

"I'm on!" said Snoop.

Two others fellows were "on" by the time the bell rang for third school. Hazel was quite keen, and Micky Desmond keener. Hazel, who was hard up as usual, preferred tea at Popper Court to tea in Hall; and Micky looked on it chiefly as a tremendous lark. Neither would have dreamed of playing a leading part; but Bolsover, under Skinner's artful persuasion, had consented to take the title-role, so to speak. Bolsover, certainly, was running a risk, though his dense brain did not quite realise it. The other fellows ran much less risk—and a spread with a baronet was worth it.

Billy Bunter had not yet heard that his problem had been solved; and he was a worried Bunter during third school. But when the Remove came out after that lesson, which was the last for the day, the afternoon being a half-holiday, Bunter heard.

His fat face brightened at the news.

Bunter, for once, was thinking less of the feed than of other considerations. His chief desire was to keep Sir Hilton Popper from inquiring into the identity of the fellow who had talked on the telephone as Coker. Still, the feed was very attractive to Bunter.

"Don't you fellows wish you were coming?" grinned the fat Owl, coming on the Famous Five in the quad.

"Where, fathead?" asked Harry.

"Tea at Popper Court!" grinned Bunter. "I'd have taken you chaps, if you'd been a bit more civil. Now I jolly well won't!"

"You've found somebody?" exclaimed Bob Cherry.

"Bolsover's got more pluck than you, Cherry!" jeered Bunter. "He's not funking it."

"The silly ass!" exclaimed Harry Wharton. "Look here, Bunter, you jolly well ought to let Coker know about old Popper asking him——"

"I'll watch it!" grinned Bunter.

"Coker ought to be told!" said Johnny Bull.

"Are you going to tell him?" sneered Bunter. "I can tell you that if you jolly well give me away to Coker——"

"Don't be a silly Owl!" snapped the captain of the Remove. "Nobody's going to give you away. But you ought to tell Coker about it, and wash out this fatheaded stunt."

"I don't think!" grinned Bunter.

"You never do!" assented Bob Cherry.

"Yah!"

By dinner-time the "stunt" was the talk of the Remove. Hitherto, Bunter's wonderful wheeze had been a joke in the Form; nobody had supposed that any fellow would be ass enough to think of playing such a game on Sir Hilton Popper. Now it was known that Bolsover major had taken it on, and some fellows wondered at his nerve, and others at his fatheadedness.

Fellows who noticed Coker of the Fifth stalking in the quad, with his usual air of being monarch of all he surveyed, wondered what the great Horace would have said if he had known.

Anyhow, Coker knew nothing, and, as far as could be seen, was not likely to know anything. All the Remove knew, and some of them disapproved of the stunt, but no fellow in the Remove had any idea of giving away the game. Coker was making his plans for that afternoon, but his plans certainly did not include tea with Sir Hilton Popper.

"I say, you fellows!"

Harry Wharton & Co. smiled.

Billy Bunter came out of the House, in the sunny June afternoon, looking quite a new Bunter.

He was spick and span, from head to foot, evidently considering that it was necessary to put on a little style when he was going to tea with a baronet.

Bunter was not often either spick or span. Generally, he was grubby, his elbows shiny, and his knees baggy. Mr. Quelch had even been known to send him out of the Form-room for a wash!

Quelch, had he seen him at this moment, would not have thought Bunter the most slovenly fellow in the Remove.

He had washed since dinner; and two washes, in one day was rather a record for Bunter. Nobody, looking at Bunter now, could have guessed what he had had for dinner. As a rule, there were clues.

His trousers had been brushed. His shoes were brightly polished. His cuffs were spotless—which hinted that the shirt was not Bunter's own. The handkerchief that jutted from his pocket was white as the driven snow—also evidence that it was not Bunter's. His tie was new and neat, and the Famous Five wondered whose it was. A handsome straw hat surmounted his bullet head—and it was just as well for Bunter that Lord Mauleverer was not on the spot to recognise it.

Bunter was looking pleased with himself. He had been looking in the glass, and in the glass he saw reflected a handsome, well-dressed, well-set-up fellow, whose spectacles rather added to his distinguished appearance. Naturally, Bunter was pleased.

He blinked at the chums of the Remove through those spectacles. His manner had a touch of patronage.

"I say, sorry I can't take you chaps!" he said. "But it would hardly do, would it?"

"Fathead!"

"What I mean is, old Popper's a crusty old stick, and a bit of an old blighter, but, after all, he's a baronet, and he's got a nobby place!" said Bunter. "Butler, and footmen, and all that! A fellow has to be a bit particular."

"You howling ass!"

"Yah!"

Bunter rolled on, disdainful.

"What about squashing that hat on his silly head?" asked Johnny Bull.

Harry Wharton laughed.

"Don't!" he said. "Mauly would have to buy a new one."

"Ha, ha, ha!"

Bolsover major came out, with Skinner and Snoop, Hazel, and Micky Desmond. All of them had rather a newly swept and garnished look. Tea with a baronet did not happen every day, and there had been a considerable amount of brushing and polishing.

Quite a crowd of the Remove gathered round to see them start. The party for Popper Court was the centre of interest in the Remove that afternoon.

Some of the fellows thought that Bolsover's nerve would fail him when the time came to start. But this did not look like it. Evidently, he was going.

Bolsover gave the captain of the Remove a nod.

"Like to come, Wharton?" he asked generously.

"Thanks, no."

"We could cram in one more, if you like!"

"I'm not anxious to sample old Popper's boot, thanks!" answered the captain of the Remove, with a laugh.

F

"The bootfulness may be terrific!" grinned Hurree Jamset Ram Singh.

"Oh, that's rot!" said Bolsover major. "It's safe as houses. Skinner jolly well wouldn't be going if it wasn't."

"Thanks!" said Skinner.

"Well, you know you wouldn't!" said Bolsover. "It's all right, Wharton, if you'd like to join up. Dash it all, I'll take the lot of you, if you like! I don't see that old Popper could object, after saying that a chap could take friends with him."

"Why not take all the Remove?" grinned Bob Cherry. "Ha, ha, ha!"

"Look here, Bolsover, you're a silly ass!" said Harry. "The best thing you can do is to wash it out. It looks safe enough, but you never can tell, and if old Popper spotted you——"

"How could he?"

"Well, I don't see how he could!" admitted Wharton. "But——"

"The butfulness is terrific."

"Oh, rot!" said Hazel. "It's right as rain! Nothing could happen unless Coker walked into Popper Court this afternoon. Is he likely to?"

"Hardly! But——"

"Oh, come on!" said Snoop.

The Popper Court party walked on, most of the Remove following them down to the gates. They walked out of the gates, grinning faces watching them as they went. Billy Bunter turned back to the Famous Five.

"I say, you fellows," he squeaked. "Look here, you can come, if you like. I'll tell you what! If I stand you a tea at Popper Court, you stand supper in the study to-night. That's fair! What about it?"

"Fathead!"

"Beast!"

Bunter rolled on.

"Come on," said Bob Cherry. "Let's see them as far as Popper Court. They may come out suddenly, and want picking up and carrying home."

"Ha, ha, ha!"

A dozen Remove fellows walked after the party, curious to see them to their destination, and to see what happened when they arrived there.

Bolsover & Co. marched up the road and turned into Oak Lane, by Courtfield Common, on which the great gates of Popper Court opened.

It was past three o'clock now, and no doubt Sir Hilton Popper was expecting his visitors.

"Hallo, hallo, hallo!" murmured Bob Cherry. "There's the old bean!"

The Popper Court gates stood open. In the gateway an eyeglass gleamed, screwed in the eye of Sir Hilton Popper.

The lord of Popper Court was standing there looking out into the lane.

Harry Wharton & Co. came to a halt. From a little distance they watched Bolsover's party walk up to the gates.

They noticed that the party slowed down a little. Perhaps some of them felt a slight misgiving at the sight of the tall, angular baronet, with his mastiff face and gleaming eyeglass.

But Bolsover major marched resolutely on. Bolsover, at all events, was not to be daunted.

"He's doing it!" murmured Bob.

"He is—he are!" grinned Nugent.

Sir Hilton scanned the party as they came up. Bolsover major marched resolutely ahead, Micky Desmond close to him, Hazel and Skinner and Snoop a little behind, and Billy Bunter bringing up the rear. Bunter, at that moment, had an awful recollection of dropping on Sir Hilton's head, a couple of days ago, and a dreadful misgiving that Sir Hilton, after all, might know who it was that had dropped on his head.

But Sir Hilton was smiling!

Smiling was a rather unaccustomed performance for Sir Hilton Popper. His old brown, leathery face broke up into a thousand wrinkles as he smiled. Still, he did smile.

This, he knew, was the party he was expecting. Perhaps he had not expected it to be quite so numerous. He had said three or four over the telephone—and six were arriving. He had no doubt that the tallest fellow, who towered over the others, was Coker. What else was Sir Hilton to think?

Anyway, they had arrived.

"Coker, what—what?"

Sir Hilton's bark reached the ears of the onlookers down the road. They exchanged grinning glances.

"Yes, sir!" said Bolsover major calmly. Really, Bolsover's nerve was quite admirable at that moment. "I've brought a few friends with me, sir, as you said I might——"

"Quite—quite!" said Sir Hilton genially. "Oh, quite! I am very glad to see you, Coker!"

He shook hands with Bolsover major.

"Very glad to see you! I have to thank you, Coker, for a great service—a very great service——"

"Not at all, sir!" said Bolsover major.

"Come in—come in!" Sir Hilton did not shake hands with the rest of the party but he gave them a genial nod as they raised their hats. "Come in—you and your friends! I am—hum—delighted to see you! Yes—hum—delighted!"

Bolsover major walked up the drive with Sir Hilton Popper. The party walked on behind.

"Well!" said Bob Cherry, as they disappeared.

"Well!" murmured Nugent.

"Looks all right!" he remarked. "I hope to goodness they'll get by with it. If old Popper smells a mouse, they're for it!"

The Famous Five walked past the gates a few minutes later. Bolsover's party had disappeared up the drive with Sir Hilton Popper. All, it seemed, was going well. And though the chums of the Remove did not quite approve of leg-pulling to such a very remarkable extent, they certainly hoped that Bolsover & Co, would pull through safely, as they walked on towards the banks of the Sark.

132

"Cheeky old ass!" said Coker.

"Yes—but——" murmured Potter.

"But——" murmured Greene.

Coker snorted.

Coker of the Fifth had been making his plans for that half-holiday. Those plans certainly did not include anything like tea with the baronet at Popper Court. But they included Potter and Greene—and those two youths did not seem overjoyed at the prospect.

"The man's a cheeky old ass!" repeated Coker. "Somebody ought to go to law with him about it. That island in the Sark belongs to him no more than it belongs to me, or to you, Potter. All very well to keep fags off it—untidy little beasts! But to bar off senior men of Greyfriars is cheek—sheer pure, unadulterated cheek!" said Coker categorically.

"I know!" said Potter soothingly. "But——"

"The Head," said Coker, "put that island out of school bounds. Why? Just because old Popper is a governor of the school and he doesn't want any trouble with a governor."

"Headmasters don't!" remarked Greene.

"Well," said Coker. "I'm not a headmaster and I don't care a brass button. Last week Prout jawed me about it. You heard him! Well I jolly well said I'd go on that island, and I jolly well did!"

"What about Lantham this afternoon?" asked Potter. "There is a good cricket match there—"

"Never mind that, Potter! Do you know what I saw when I was on Popper's Island that day last week?"

"You saw old Popper's silver pots and——"

"I don't mean that, ass! I saw a board up: 'Trespassers will be Prosecuted,'" said Coker. "Mind, that island is public land. Every chap in the kingdom has a perfect right to land on that island, and stop on it as long as he jolly well likes! And that old curmudgeon has the nerve—the cheek—the impudence—to stick up a board saying that trespassers will be prosecuted! The neck!"

Coker of the Fifth breathed indignation.

133

"And speaking of those silver pots," he went on. "I found the stuff hidden under the willows—jolly well banged my head on it when I went over in the mud—mightn't have found it otherwise. What are you grinning at, you silly asses?"

"Oh, nothing! I say, what about getting down to Pegg, and having a boat out on the bay——"

"I'm speaking, Potter. If you must jaw you might give a fellow a chance to get a word in edge-wise. What has old Popper done about my finding his silver pots?" demanded Coker. "I'm not the fellow to do a song and dance about it, I suppose—but that stuff was worth hundreds of pounds, and I got it back for the old ass. Has he said a word about it?"

Coker snorted.

"He might thank a chap!" he said. "He might mention that he's obliged. Not a word! I suppose he thinks I'm a sort of manservant, and it's my business to pick up his silver pots when they're lying about. Might have expected me to clean 'em, before sending them back, as they'd been in the mud!" added Coker with deadly sarcasm.

"Well, he might have said something about it," admitted Potter. "I'm rather surprised that he hasn't. He must have been pleased at getting the Popper Court silver home again."

"I should jolly well think he might," said Coker scornfully. "If he's too high-and-mighty to walk over to the school, he could have rung up on the phone, and said as much as 'Thank you!' Has he?"

"Well, he always was a crusty old stick!" said Greene. "Can't expect much from him in the way of manners."

Another snort from Coker.

Not a word had come from him—so far as Coker knew, at all events. Coker, as he said, was not the fellow to do a song and dance about it—but he did feel rather sore at such a service passing without a single word of recognition or acknowledgment.

If the lord of Popper Court fancied that the whole population of the kingdom existed for no purpose but to do

134

At Popper Court!

SIR HILTON POPPER smiled.

It cost him, perhaps, something of an effort to keep smiling. It was so very new an experience for him. But he did it.

Some elderly gentlemen feel bucked in the presence of cheery boyhood. But Sir Hilton was not one of that kind. He regarded boys as troublesome animals, and the less he saw of them the better he liked them. So it really was much to Sir Hilton's credit that he was making the effort, to testify the obligation he felt towards Coker of the Greyfriars Fifth. Far from being unmindful of Coker's service, as Coker had reason to suppose, Sir Hilton was going all out to acknowledge it—though unfortunately in the wrong quarter.

Some of the party had felt a twinge of uneasiness at first, but that soon passed off.

Sir Hilton was absolutely unsuspicious. It could hardly have entered his lofty and lordly mind at any time, that any fellow would dream of pulling his lofty and lordly leg. And there was nothing to make him suspicious now. He was expecting a party of Greyfriars boys—and a party of Greyfriars boys had arrived. He was expecting to see a big fellow called Coker—and he was seeing a big fellow called Coker! How was Sir Hilton to suspect that that big fellow, on other occasions, was called Percy Bolsover? Of course, he could not.

Little tables were set out under the branches of a big, shady oak. Menservants were carrying things down from the house to those little tables. Billy Bunter's eyes, and spectacles, were on them. Bunter could see that it was going to be a good tea. He thought it rather a mistake not to have had it at once. But apart from that, Bunter was satisfied.

What to do with a party of schoolboys was a little bit of a problem to the lord of Popper Court. He remembered, from his own distant boyhood, that eatables would surely be welcome. Eatables and drinkables had been provided in abundance—if not superabundance.

But the whole visit could not be filled up with eating and drinking—though that programme would have satisfied Bunter, at least. Tea was not due till four o'clock, which was quite early.

Sir Hilton smiled resolutely; and Bolsover & Co. had their best party grins on. But a whole hour could not be passed standing on the lawn smiling and grinning.

"Tennis, what?" suggested Sir Hilton brightly.

Nobody had brought a racket. But it was easy to fix the party up with rackets. Sir Hilton sent a man into the house to sort out rackets.

Bolsover major did not play tennis. Neither did Snoop. Hazel, Skinner, and Micky Desmond did, and Billy Bunter fancied he did. So four of them were disposed of.

The other two watched with Sir Hilton. Billy Bunter paired off with Hazel, Skinner with Micky.

"Rotten court!" remarked Bunter to Hazel, perhaps unaware that the remark reached Sir Hilton's ears. When Bunter played tennis, he generally remarked that it was a rotten court. The rottenness of the court accounted for the rotten play Bunter displayed thereon.

"Shut up, you ass!" whispered Hazel.

"We've something better than this at Bunter Court," said the fat Owl, unheeding, "I hate these rotten old grass courts."

Bolsover major and Snoop, standing on either side of Sir Hilton Popper, exchanged a wink behind his ramrod back.

The expression on Sir Hilton's face at that moment, entertained them. His eye gleamed through his eyeglass at Bunter.

"Service!" called out Micky from the other end.

Bunter took the service.

He did not take it with his racket. Micky had a fast service, and the ball came down like a bullet. It was doubtful whether Bunter saw it at all. He flailed the air with his racket, what time the ball bounced up and landed on a fat chin.

"Yaroooh!" roared Bunter.

He sat down.

He sat down suddenly and hard, and it was perhaps just as well for Bunter that it was one of those rotten old grass courts, and not a hard court. Even the grass felt hard as he jammed on it with all his weight.

Bump!

"Yoo-hoo-hoop!"

Bunter dropped his racket and caressed a podgy chin which felt as if it had been pushed through his podgy head.

"Yow-ow-ow-ow!" squeaked Bunter, "Beast! Wow!"

"Ha, ha, ha!"

"Ow! My chin! Ow!"

"Fifteen—love!" chortled Bolsover major. "Is that how you play tennis at Bunter Court, old fat man?"

"Ow! Beast! Wow!"

Bunter staggered up. He rubbed his chin, and set his glasses straight on his fat little nose. Micky and Skinner, grinning, changed courts, and Micky brandished his racket again.

"Service!"

Hazel returned the ball and it came back from Skinner. To and fro it went. For a minute or two, Hazel played a single game, while Bunter rubbed his chin. But the fat Owl was not going to be left out, and he gripped his racket and rushed into the fray again, as the ball came over from Micky.

"Look out, Hazel!" yelled Bolsover major.

But it was too late.

Hazel and Bunter got the ball together. Hazel lifted it back neatly over the net. Bunter's swipe missed it by

139

a foot. But every bullet has its billet; and that swipe found a resting place. Hazel let out a fearful yell as Bunter's racket cracked on his ear.

"Whooooop!"

"Ha, ha, ha!" shrieked Bolsover major. "Bravo, Bunter!"

"Oh, crikey!" howled Hazel, staggering. "Ow! Ow! My ear! My napper! You mad porpoise——ow!"

"You silly ass!" hooted Bunter. "That was my shot!"

"You mad rhinoceros——ow!"

"Thirty—love!" chanted Bolsover major, as the ball dropped unheeded.

"Ha, ha, ha!"

"Yaroooh!" roared Bunter as Hazel whirled on him with uplifted racket, and smote. "Ow! Keep off! Wharrer you up to? Oh, crikey! Ow!"

Swipe, swipe, swipe!

Hazel, for the moment, seemed to have forgotten that he was playing tennis, and fancied that he was playing Bunter!

Swipe, swipe!

"You'll damage that racket, Hazel!" yelled Snoop.

"You'll damage Bunter!" chortled Bolsover major.

"Ha, ha, ha!"

"Yarooooh! I say, you fellows—whoop!" howled Bunter, as he dodged frantically. "I say—yaroooh!"

"There!" gasped Hazel. "There, you mad ass—there, you fat lunatic—there, you blithering cuckoo——"

"Ow! Beast! Wow!"

"Ha, ha, ha!"

"Service!" roared Micky.

Hazel, glowering, retired to his court. Billy Bunter, gasping for breath, picked up his racket. Bunter was not enjoying this game. However, he prepared to take the service again.

Down came the ball, and this time Bunter got it. It was rather unusual for Bunter's racket to establish contact with the ball at all. When it did, the direction to be taken by the ball was quite an unknown quantity. It might have

140

gone back across the net by a lucky chance, but with so many points of the compass to choose from, it was more likely that it wouldn't! On this occasion, it didn't!

Bunter swiped that ball, and it whizzed. For a fraction of a second nobody knew the flight of the ball.

Then a fiendish yell from Sir Hilton Popper announced where it had gone. The lord of Popper Court was seen to stagger and clasp a hand to his nose. The ball dropped at his feet.

"Oh, crikey!" gasped Bolsover major.

"Oh, crumbs!" gurgled Snoop.

"Good gad! Oooooogh!" spluttered Sir Hilton. "What —what—what—urrggh! What—what—gurrrgggh!"

Billy Bunter blinked around.

"I say, you fellows, where's that ball? I say, did it go over the net? I say, has it gone off the court?"

"Ha, ha, ha!"

"Gurrrrggh!" gurgled Sir Hilton clasping an anguished nose. "Wurrggh! You dangerous young rascal—urrggh!"

"Oh, crikey!" gasped Bunter, as he realised where the ball had gone. "Oh, jiminy! I—I say, you keep off!"

Sir Hilton was making an infuriated stride towards him. With that sudden, severe pain in his nose, the baronet seemed to forget, for a moment, that Bunter was a guest. He strode at him with an expression on his face that made the fat Owl jump.

"Oh!" gasped Bunter, and he bolted.

Between his short sight, and the haste of the moment, Bunter forgot the net. He was reminded of it, however, as he crashed headlong into it, stumbled, and hung over it.

"Ha, ha, ha!"

"Ow! Groogh! Wow!" roared Bunter, wriggling. "I say, you keep off! Oooop!"

Fortunately, Sir Hilton remembered in time! He gave an angry snort and strode off the tennis court.

Billy Bunter disentangled himself from the net, and blinked round through his big spectacles.

"I—I say, is that beast gone? Oh, dear! Ill-tempered

141

old beast, you know—ooooh! Blessed if I see anything to cackle at!''

"Ha, ha, ha!"

That set finished without the presence of Sir Hilton Popper. He seemed to have had enough of Bunter's tennis at close quarters.

It was with the greatest difficulty that Sir Hilton summoned up a smile when the juniors came back to the lawn, Sir Hilton's nose, like Marian's in the ballad, was red and raw. It had a pain in it.

But it was time for tea now. Billy Bunter cast a blink of the deepest appreciation at the tables under the shady oak. Tennis, perhaps, was not Bunter's game, but when it came to shifting the foodstuffs, Bunter was in a class by himself.

"I say, you fellows, the grub's all right!" murmured Bunter.

When the grub was all right, everything was all right. The grub, undoubtedly, was all right; three or four menservants hovered about, to wait on the guests. Sir Hilton smiled with resolute hospitality, occasionally caressing his nose. In a state of happy satisfaction, Bolsover & Co. sat down to that gorgeous spread.

"I wonder what Coker would think if he saw this!" Skinner whispered to Bolsover major.

Bolsover chuckled.

"I wonder where Coker is," he remarked, "while we're bagging his feed?"

He little guessed!

"Hallo, hallo, hallo!" ejaculated Bob Cherry.

"Coker!"

"That ass!"

"What on earth's he up to?"

Harry Wharton & Co., after seeing the Popper Court party in at Popper Court, had strolled on, down to the river. Now they were sauntering down the bank of the Sark, on the towpath that bordered Popper Court woods.

As they came in view of Popper's Island, out in the river, they came also in view of a remarkable sight.

At the landing place on that island, a post had been planted, and the post bore a large board, on which was painted a legend in large letters:

"TRESPASSERS WILL BE
PROSECUTED!"

Nobody could walk along the towpath without seeing that board on the island. It was a standing offence in the eyes of Greyfriars fellows. But certainly no Greyfriars fellow, except Horace Coker of the Fifth Form, had ever thought of pulling it down.

Coker had not only thought of it; he was doing it. At all events, he was trying his hardest to do it.

Halting on the bank, the chums of the Remove stared across at Coker of the Fifth.

A boat was tied up at the island—evidently Coker's boat. Coker was on the island. He had knotted the end of a long, strong rope to the offending board. He was pulling on that rope with all his ample beef. His rugged face was red with exertion. If Coker's beef could do it, that board was coming down.

They gazed at him.

"The blithering ass!" breathed Harry. "He may be spotted any minute. If a keeper came out of the wood——"

"Asking for it!" said Johnny Bull.

"The askfulness is terrific!"

The juniors glanced round uneasily. The sweeping woods lay along the river with a dozen little dusky paths winding into the trees. From any one of them, at any moment, keepers might have emerged? Evidently Coker feared no foe! For the moment, however, the Famous Five had the river bank to themselves.

"Coker!" called out Wharton.

Horace Coker ceased his herculean efforts for a moment

and stared round. He had not noticed, till that moment, that he had an audience.

Beefy as Horace was, he had not, so far, made an impression on the post or the board. He needed, as he had told Potter and Greene, help.

"For goodness' sake, Coker, get off that island!" called out the captain of the Remove. "I saw Joyce in the wood not ten minutes ago."

"Don't be cheeky!" answered Coker.

"You'll be nabbed!" exclaimed Nugent.

"Who cares?"

Coker, clearly, did not care! At all events, he was prepared to risk it.

"You fags cut off!" called out Coker. "Hold on, though!" he added. "You can lend me a hand if you like! It's a bit tough for one fellow. I expected Potter and Greene to come along, but the silly asses went wandering off somewhere."

"Couldn't follow a better example!" grinned Bob Cherry. "We'd better wander off somewhere, too, you fellows—and so had you, Coker!"

"Don't be a young idiot!" said Coker. "I'm getting this cheeky board down! The other fellows can stand old Popper's impudence if they like! I'm not taking any! I'll bring the rope across, and you can all pull——"

"Fathead!"

"Funky?" sneered Coker. "Well, if you're funky, you little rotters, clear off, before I come over and kick you!"

"Chuck it, you ass!" exclaimed Harry. "You'll get into a fearful row."

Coker did not even answer.

He grasped the rope, braced himself for a tug, and tugged. He tugged hard, but the offending board did not give. Beefy as Coker was, he had set himself a task rather beyond his powers.

The juniors watched him anxiously. Coker, it was clear, was not going to chuck it till he had that board down. At his present rate of progress, he seemed likely to be busy all the afternoon. Harry Wharton cast another anxious

Cra-a-ack! There was a rending sound as the board parted company with the post

glance along the border of the wood, and then looked at his comrades.

"After all, it's like old Popper's cheek to stick that board up!" he said. "And that blithering idiot is for it if he's caught. And he will be caught."

"Let's!" said Bob.

"Coker!" called out Harry.

"Shut up!" came over Coker's shoulder as he tugged. "Bring the rope over, and we'll help!"

Coker gasped.

"Oh, all right!"

Whether Coker could have done it on his own or not, he was going to do it! At least, he was going on trying to do it! But undoubtedly he was glad of help. Five sturdy arms pulling on the rope would easily make all the difference. Coker was very glad of help.

He ceased to tug, and threw the end of the rope into his boat. Then he jumped into the boat, and punted it across the channel between the island and the bank.

He stepped out of the boat to the towpath, the end of the rope in his hand.

"Here you are!" gasped Coker.

He was rather short of breath. He had expended a great deal before the Famous Five happened on him.

"Line up!" said Harry Wharton. "Quick as you can, you fellows!"

"There's no hurry!" remarked Coker. "Take your time!"

"The hurryfulness is terrific, my esteemed Coker!" said Hurree Jamset Ram Singh. "If some absurd keeper comes out of the wood——"

"Rot!" said Coker.

"They keep an eye on this island, fathead!" said Bob.

"Let them!" said Coker disdainfully. "If any keeper starts bothering me, I shall hit him. I'm not standing any nonsense from old Popper, or from his keepers, either, I can tell you!"

"Well, we're not looking for a scrap with keepers!" said the captain of the Remove, laughing. "You may like a flogging from the Head, Coker, but we should hate it!"

"Don't be a cheeky young ass, Wharton! Look here——"

"Nuff said!" interjected Bob Cherry. "Get going, you men!"

The Famous Five grasped the rope, one behind another, as if for a tug-o'-war. Horace Coker took the end.

"Now pull!" said Coker. "Don't jaw—pull!"

The five juniors braced themselves and pulled. They set their feet firmly in the grassy bank, grasping the rope with both hands, and exerted all their strength. Coker, at the end of the rope, put all his beef and weight into it. The rope stretched taut across the arm of the river, from the board on the island, to the tugging crowd on the bank.

That it was a task beyond Coker's solitary powers was clear—for the well-planted post resisted the efforts of the whole six.

They tugged, and tugged, and tugged.

For a whole minute there was no result. When the result came, it came suddenly.

The post on the island did not stir. But the board came off it, dragged bodily away by the dragging rope.

It flew off the post, and flew into the river with a splash. And the sudden easing of the rope sent the tugging party stumbling headlong backwards.

Coker went over on his back, and over Coker went the Famous Five, sprawling. There was a loud roar from Coker as he squashed into the grass, with five Removites distributed over him.

"Oh! Ow! Gerroff! You clumsy young asses! Oh!"

"Oh, my hat!" gasped Bob Cherry.

"Oh crumbs!"

The juniors scrambled up breathlessly. Coker sat up in the grass and gurgled for breath.

"Urrggh! You clumsy little idiots! Oooogh!" he gurgled. "I've a jolly good mind to kick you all the way back to the school! Urrgh!"

"That's Coker's way of saying 'Thank you!'" remarked

Bob Cherry. "The speech may be taken as read, Coker!"

"Ha, ha, ha!"

"Well, we've jolly well done it!" remarked Johnny Bull, as he pulled the rope, and the "Trespassers" board came bumping into the rushes. "And now we've done it, the sooner we do the vanishing trick, the better."

"Yes, rather."

"Untie that rope," said Coker. "I've got to take that back! We'll leave the board here for old Popper to see next time he takes a walk this way! And—and——"

"Oh, crikey!" ejaculated Bob Cherry. "Look!"

From the wood, a little distance above the spot where the juniors stood, a man in gaiters and velveteens emerged into view. The juniors knew Joyce, the head keeper of Popper Court.

"Hook it!" breathed Nugent.

But there was no chance of "hooking" it. From the wood below the spot two more figures emerged, almost at the same moment.

The juniors looked up the bank, at Joyce, and down the bank, at the other two keepers. And Bob Cherry grunted:

"Copped!"

And Hurree Jamset Ram Singh added sadly that the copfulness was terrific!

Held by the Enemy!

HORACE COKER breathed hard, his eyes gleamed, as the keepers converged on the spot. His big fists were clenched. Three hefty keepers were more than a match for Coker and the juniors; but Coker, as usual, feared no foe and counted no odds.

Obviously, he was preparing to knock Joyce & Co. into the middle of next week, or the whole length of the calendar, if they ventured to lay disrespectful hands on him. Which, equally obviously, they certainly were going to do.

The trespassers board, broken from its post on the island, lay in the rushes by the bank.

That was enough for Sir Hilton's keepers. But Joyce touched his hat as he came up.

"Sorry, young gentlemen," he said; "but I shall have to ask you to come along with me! You pulled down that there board."

"Sort of!" assented Bob Cherry.

"We shall have to take you to Sir Hilton," said Joyce. "But I dessay he will only take your names, to send to your headmaster, sir."

Harry Wharton & Co. nodded dismally. They could really have kicked themselves. They had lent Horace a hand to hurry on his proceedings, to keep him out of a scrape. Instead of keeping Coker out of a scrape they had tumbled into one themselves—and a very serious one.

But they were not, like Coker, thinking of punching a way out. Pulling down Sir Hilton's board was enough to earn them a flogging at Greyfriars. Punching his keepers certainly would not improve matters. It was more likely to have the effect of turning a flogging into the "sack."

But Coker did not think of that. Coker was no whale
on thinking. Action was more in his line.

"Hands off, you!" snapped Coker. "If you want me to
knock you into the river, you've only got to say so!"

"You'd better come quiet, sir!" said Joyce. "You
pulled down that there board——"

"I'll pull it down again if that old ass Popper has the
neck to stick it up again!" retorted Coker. "And if you
lay a finger on me, I'll knock you spinning!"

"Coker——"

"Shut up, Wharton!"

Joyce eyed Coker dubiously. He gave a whistle, and
there was a rustle in the wood. Two more keepers
emerged.

Five hefty men in velveteens surrounded the Greyfriars
party now. Resistance was hopeless, even if it could have
led to anything but making matters worse. But that made
no difference to Horace Coker.

Joyce touched him on the arm.

"Hands off!" roared Coker.

"Better come quietly, sir," said the head keeper. "You
see—— Yaroooh! Oh—— Oooooogh!"

Coker hit out.

Joyce rolled over on the bank, under a hefty smite,
roaring.

"Coker, you ass——" gasped Bob.

"Back up, you fags!" roared Coker.

And he rushed at the keepers, his sinewy arms going
like the sails of a windmill!

Instantly he was collared, and a terrific struggle followed. Coker staggered right and left, struggling, punching,
and spluttering. Joyce scrambled up—his good temper
gone, and replaced by an extremely bad temper.

"Collar them!" he shouted.

Coker struggled wildly. The juniors stood nonplussed.
Coker, as usual, was playing the goat; but to stand idly
by while he struggled in the grasp of the keepers, did not
seem good to the Famous Five.

Bob Cherry, forgetting prudence, rushed in to help Coker. He knocked one of the keepers backwards.

That was enough for the Co. With one accord they piled in. Prudence was thrown to the winds, and they backed up Coker with might and main.

For two or three minutes there was wild trampling and struggling and panting on the towpath.

Then Coker of the Fifth was pinned, a keeper's grip on either arm, and he wrenched and wrestled in vain to free himself.

"Leggo!" roared Coker. "I'll smash you! I'll spiflicate you! Will you leggo?"

But the keepers did not let go. They gripped hard and fast, and the hefty Horace was reduced to helplessness. He still struggled and spluttered, but they had him safe.

At the same time, Joyce got Nugent and Hurree Singh by their collars, and held on. Another keeper secured Bob Cherry. The other was hotly engaged with Wharton and Johnny Bull. They could have got away—but they had no idea of leaving their comrades in the lurch. And it was clear now, even to Coker, that punching a way out was a chicken that would not fight.

"Chuck it, you chaps!" gasped Bob. "The game's up!"

And Wharton and Johnny Bull "chucked" it.

"You young rascals!" gasped Joyce. "You're all going before Sir Hilton, and I 'ope your 'eadmaster will wallop you when you're sent back. Bring that fellow along!"

"Leggo!" roared Coker.

He resisted manfully. But the two men grasping his arms hooked him along, and he had to go. They did not relax their grasp on Coker for a moment. Coker, evidently, was going to be dangerous if he got loose.

"Now, you young rascals, come along!" said Joyce gruffly. And, with the other two keepers, he shepherded the Famous Five into the wood after Coker.

"Oh, crumbs!" mumbled Bob, dabbing his nose as he went. "What an afternoon! We've asked for this!"

"The askfulness was preposterous!" mumbled the Nabob of Bhanipur.

The party followed a winding path through the woods, leading to Popper Court. Coker raged as he went, still full of beans. But the Famous Five went with glum faces. They were booked for a fearful row, and they knew it; and they hardly ventured to contemplate what their headmaster would say, and do, when they were sent back to the school—perhaps conducted there by Sir Hilton Popper in person!

They emerged from the wood at last, and Popper Court lay in sight in the distance.

The keepers marched them on, Coker still wriggling, and demanding to be "leggo."

As they approached the mansion, the juniors spotted a number of figures on the lawn before the house.

One of them was a tall, angular figure, with an eyeglass screwed in an eye. Others were menservants moving to and fro. And gathered at some little tables under a shady oak, were half a dozen schoolboys.

"Oh, crikey!" gasped Bob. The Famous Five had forgotten about the Popper Court party. Now they were reminded of it.

They were being marched into the presence of Sir Hilton Popper—and of Bolsover & Co.

As they came towards the lawn, convoyed by the keepers, Sir Hilton's eyes turned on them in surprise—deepening to wrath.

The Popper Court party were sitting down to tea. Sir Hilton had screwed up his tough features into a genial, hospitable grin. But that genial grin vanished now, as if wiped off by a duster.

It was replaced by the grimmest of frowns.

"What is this?" he barked. "Trespassers, what? By gad! Are those boys trespassers, Joyce?"

And he strode to meet them, with an expression on his face that might have excited the envy of the fabled Gorgon! And the Popper Court party, all on their feet now, forgot the spread they had been about to sample— even Billy Bunter forgot it—as they stared at the captured trespassers.

"Oh, crikey!" gasped Bolsover major. "That—that—that—that's Coker!"

Sir Hilton Popper fixed his eyes, and his eyeglass, on the new arrivals.

Harry Wharton & Co. stood silent. They were "for it" now, and they could only make up their minds to take what was coming to them as philosophically as possible.

Not so Coker! Coker, as full of beans as ever, glared defiance. He knew Sir Hilton by sight, if Sir Hilton did not know him. And he glared at Sir Hilton with undiminished truculence.

"Who are these boys, Joyce?" thundered Sir Hilton. "Have you caught them trespassing?"

"Yes, sir!" said Joyce. "They've pulled down the board on the island, Sir Hilton!"

"Pip-pip-pulled down the bib-bib-board!" Sir Hilton fairly stuttered, in his astonishment and wrath. "Pip-pulled down my bib-board! Are you serious, Joyce? Is is possible? Gad!"

"And I'll jolly well pull it down again!" roared Coker of the Fifth. "Who are you to stick up a board?"

"What?" gasped Sir Hilton. "What?"

"Who are you?" bawled Coker.

"Good gad!"

"If you want to know what I think of you——"

"Shut up, you ass!" gasped Harry Wharton. "For the love of Mike, shut up! Do you hear? Shut up!"

"Good gad!" repeated Sir Hilton. "Greyfriars boys—by gad! I know some of them—I've seen them before! Pulling down by board! Good gad! I'll have them flogged! I'll have them expelled! By gad! I'll——"

"Oh, chuck it!" interjected Coker.

"What! What did you say?" gasped the lord of Popper Court. Probably Sir Hilton Popper, in all his lordly career, had never before been bidden to "chuck it."

"I said chuck it!" retorted Coker. "Who are you, I'd like to know? Think you're the Great Panjandrum? Yah!"

"Who—who—who am I?" gasped Sir Hilton. "By

153

Jove! I'll very soon let you know, you impudent young scoundrel! And I'm going to know who you are! I'm going to demand your expulsion from Greyfriars. Do you hear? If I'm a governor of the school, by gad, I——"

"Rats!" retorted Coker.

"Wha-a-at?"

"Rats!"

"Good gad! If I had my riding-whip here, I'd lay it about you! By gad! James, fetch my riding-whip! Do you hear? Fetch it at once!"

"Yes, Sir Hilton!" gasped James, scuttling off.

"Now, your name?" bawled Sir Hilton. "Your name, you impudent young rascal?"

"Think I'm afraid to tell you my name?" bawled Coker. "You're welcome to hear it, if you want to! My name's Coker, and a better name than Popper any day!"

Sir Hilton gave a start.

"Coker?" he repeated.

"C-O-K-E-R, Coker!" retorted Horace. "Like me to spell it for you? Coker! Got it? Coker!"

"Coker? Nonsense! Your name is not Coker! How dare you pretend that you are Coker, when Coker is here!" thundered Sir Hilton Popper.

"Eh?"

"How dare you!" roared Sir Hilton. "No doubt you fancy you may get off lightly by pretending that you are Coker, as I am under an obligation to the boy Coker! But I see through your trickery. Coker is here, at this very moment!"

Horace gazed at him. He forgot his wrath in his amazement.

"Potty, or what?" he asked. "My name's Coker! Ask your man Joyce—he knows my name well enough!"

"Joyce! What is this boy's name?"

"Coker, sir!" answered Joyce.

"Impossible! Nonsense! Coker is here! Coker is my guest this afternoon. I was speaking to Coker only a few minutes ago! Coker! Come here, Coker!" Sir Hilton glanced round at the tea party under the oak.

154

A startling sight met his view.

As soon as the name of Coker was mentioned, it was quite clear to the Popper Court party that the game was up. Nothing could have given the imposture away, except Coker unexpectedly butting in! And here was Coker—unexpectedly butting in!

James was coming back from the house with the riding-whip! Bolsover & Co. did not need telling on whom that riding-whip was likely to be used, in these unexpected circumstances.

They bolted!

And so, as Sir Hilton looked round at the tea party, calling to the fellow he believed to be Coker, what he saw was six alarmed schoolboys bolting across the lawn.

He had only a back view of his honoured guests!

Even Billy Bunter stayed only to grab at a cake, and did not stop to take a bite at it. Cake in hand, the fat Owl fled after the others.

Like the guests in Macbeth, the guests at Popper Court stood not upon the order of their going, but went at once.

They ran like rabbits!

Sir Hilton Popper stared at their backs blankly. Harry Wharton & Co. grinned. Never had they seen a tea party break up so suddenly.

"What—what—what——" stuttered Sir Hilton Popper.

"Your riding-whip, sir," said James.

Sir Hilton took it mechanically.

"What—what——" he stuttered. "I—I fail to understand this! Who was that boy? He gave his name as Coker —he was Coker! If he was not Coker, who was he? Joyce, are you sure that this young rascal—hum!—that this young gentleman is—is—is Coker?"

"Quite, Sir Hilton."

"Your—your name is Coker?" stuttered Sir Hilton, blinking at the amazed Horace.

"Of course my name's Coker!" hooted Horace. "Mean to say that somebody else has been calling himself Coker? Rot!"

"That young rascal!" Sir Hilton pointed with his riding-whip at Bolsover major's disappearing form. "That——"

"That's Bolsover, a kid in the Remove!" snorted Coker. "What the dickens do you mean? Mean to say he made out he was me? Rot!"

Sir Hilton Popper gasped.

He was not quick on the uptake, but he could not help understanding now that his lofty leg had been pulled.

"That—that boy is not Coker; those—those boys are not Coker's friends! I have been deceived, deluded! Certainly he gave his name as Coker, and I had never seen the boy before. Good gad!"

"Well, my hat!" gasped Horace. "The cheeky young sweep! A kid in the Remove! I'll jolly well whop him! What the thump did he come here making out that he was me for?"

Harry Wharton & Co. chuckled. They knew the answer to that one, if Coker of the Fifth didn't.

"Good gad!" gasped Sir Hilton. "An impudent imposture! I—I—I——" Words failed the lord of Popper Court. He woke to sudden action.

Gripping the riding-whip, he charged across the lawn in pursuit of the fleeing tea party.

"Oh, crumbs!" gasped Harry Wharton.

"Put it on, Bunter!" roared Bob.

Bolsover & Co. had a good start. They were losing no time. But the long legs of Sir Hilton Popper seemed to cover the ground like lightning; he gained ground.

Harry Wharton & Co., from the lawn, watched the chase breathlessly. Still more breathlessly Bolsover & Co. ran for their lives. They were going down the drive in great style. But it booted not. Sir Hilton's long legs went like lightning. Bunter, rearmost of the party, gave a sudden fiendish yell as the riding-whip landed.

"Yooooop!"

The cake flew from Bunter's fat hand. He yelled and dodged. Five fellows were bunched together ahead, running wildly, but Sir Hilton was on them the next moment. The riding-whip whacked right and left.

Whack, whack, whack! Swipe, swipe, swipe!

156

Wild howls and yells rang from the hapless tea party; they dodged and jumped and howled and roared and ran.

It was quite exciting till they reached the gateway and bolted out into the road. Billy Bunter, last to escape, got the last swipe as he went, and his frantic yell echoed back. Sir Hilton Popper brandished the riding-whip after them as they vanished down the road.

"What next?" murmured Bob Cherry.

Sir Hilton, breathless, with the riding-whip tucked under his arm, came back to the lawn.

He looked at Coker. Coker looked at him. Coker was still truculent, but Sir Hilton had calmed down considerably.

"Joyce," he barked, "you may release those boys! You may go! Go at once!"

"Coker!" said Sir Hilton. "You—you are Coker! You are the Coker—I mean the boy who recovered the stolen property for me—the Popper Court silver—what?"

"What about that?" grunted Coker.

"Why did you not come here to-day? I naturally supposed that that young rascal was Coker, as he gave the name, and I was expecting you——"

"Expecting me!"

"Certainly. After speaking to you on Mr. Prout's telephone yesterday——"

"You didn't!"

"Eh?"

"I never got any call on Prout's telephone——"

"What?"

"How could I, when I was out of gates all the afternoon——"

"You—you—you did not? Good gad! Someone else must have telephoned, using your name! There has been trickery! That young rascal—— Good gad! I shall inquire into this! However——" Sir Hilton paused. "Then you did not know that I telephoned to thank you for the great service you had rendered me——"

"Oh!"

"And to ask you to come to tea here this afternoon——"

"Oh!"

"And—and——" Sir Hilton paused again. It was not
easy for him to swallow the affair of the notice-board.
But he got it down. "Coker, I am much obliged to you—
I am under a deep obligation to you! I shall overlook
your offences; I shall forget them. You are here; stay to
tea with me, you and your friends. Please sit down."

"Oh, crumbs!" said Coker.

"I am glad to see you—to make your acquaintance, my
boy! You are welcome, you and your friends. Please sit
down. James! John! William! See that these boys have
everything they want. Coker, pray sit down!"

Coker sat down.

So did Harry Wharton & Co.

It was quite a different tea party at Popper Court—
but it was quite a cheery and satisfied tea party.

"Not a bad old bean!" Coker said afterwards to Potter
and Greene.

The Popper Court party returned home in great spirits.
They found the other Popper Court party in the lowest
of spirits.

But it was all right for them.

Coker, like the good-natured fellow he was, had begged
Sir Hilton to overlook what was, Coker explained, only a
silly lark of silly fags. Sir Hilton consented to do so. So
that was that! Harry Wharton & Co. handed over the
good news, and all was well—except that Billy Bunter
still mourned for the gorgeous spread that had been so
nearly his, and which he had to narrowly missed.

And Coker, entertained and made much of at Popper
Court, revised his opinion of Sir Hilton Popper, and said
he was sorry.

ARMADA BOOKS

Armada Books are wonderful, with their gay spines adding colour to your bookshelf. Are you collecting your own library of Armada Books? A book a week . . . or a month . . and in no time you would have a marvellous collection! *Start today!* Always ask your bookseller or newsagent for Armada Books, but if you have difficulty in getting the titles you want write to Armada Books, 14 St. James's Place, London S.W.1, enclosing a postal order for 3s. or 4s., depending on the price of the book, which includes postage charges in the U.K. and Ireland. Overseas readers should write to the same address for information about their nearest stockists, etc.

BOOKS AVAILABLE INCLUDE:

Mystery and Adventure stories by
      Christine Bernard
      Enid Blyton
      John Gunn
      Captain W. E. Johns
      Ralph Hammond
      Malcolm Saville

Pony and Animal stories by
      Monica Edwards
      Ruby Ferguson
      Mary Gervaise
      Marguerite Henry
      Walt Morey
      The Pullein-Thompson sisters
      Martha Robinson
      Pat Smythe

School stories by
      Angela Brazil
      Elinor M. Brent-Dyer
      Anthony Buckeridge
      Frank Richards
      Noel Streatfeild
      Geoffrey Willans and Ronald Searle
      P. G. Wodehouse

For current stock list, please send a stamped, self-addressed envelope to Armada Books, 14 St. James's Place, London S.W.1.

COMING IN ARMADA

NOVEMBER 1970

Jennings Goes To School

by

ANTHONY BUCKERIDGE

Price 3s. 6d.